MRS. WATSON AND THE SHAKESPEARE CURSE

London, 1906: One of the world's foremost Shakespeare scholars presents a paper at Madame Tussaud's which claims that the real author of the works accredited to the Bard of Avon was none other than Queen Elizabeth I. Few in his audience, including the redoubtable Amelia Watson, wife of Doctor John H., take him seriously — but shortly afterward he is found murdered in his hotel room. Worse — Amelia's actor friend, Harry Benbow, is falsely accused of the crime. Can Amelia clear his name before Scotland Yard catch up to him?

MICHAEL MALLORY

MRS. WATSON AND THE SHAKESPEARE CURSE

Complete and Unabridged

LINFORD
Leicester

First published in Great Britain

First Linford Edition
published 2018

A catalogue record for this book is available
from the British Library.

ISBN 978–1–4448–3636–3

Published by
F. A. Thorpe (Publishing)
Anstey, Leicestershire

Set by Words & Graphics Ltd.
Anstey, Leicestershire
Printed and bound in Great Britain by
T. J. International Ltd., Padstow, Cornwall

This book is printed on acid-free paper

Prologue

Richmond Palace, London, England
1603

The flickering tallow that had dripped itself into a milky mass over the pewter candlestick gave off but scant illumination, making the process of writing all the more difficult. Exacerbating it was the fact that what light there was present was being absorbed by the colours of the ornate tapestries that adorned the walls of the great hall. What was not absorbed was the sound of the quill scritch-scratching inky words onto the foolscap; if anything, the sound was exaggerated by the cavernous room, creating in the mind of the one known to a very privileged few as 'the Poet Queen' the image of a church sexton scraping two bones together in a charnel house. *How grotesque*, the Poet Queen thought. There were times when such pearls of imagination could be saved and put to use in a future play, but this one was too grim to remember. Then again, it was hard to banish completely the spectre of death, since it hovered above the palace itself this evening.

Knowing that time was waning as rapidly as the tallow flame, the Poet Queen replenished the ink on the quill nib and continued on, silently regretting the decision to forego another classical setting. The writing of this play was not simply proving problematic; it was charted for disaster. It could not have been more doomed if it were Spain's hopes for the Armada. But the Globe had a schedule to maintain and the play had already been announced to the shareholder, and its first unsatisfactory version had already been registered with the Stationers Company. There was no way to abandon the project.

Scritch-scratch, scritch-scratch; the letters dribbled onto the paper:

> *True swains in love shall in the world*
> *   to come*
> *Approve their truth by Troilus.*
> *   When their rhymes,*
> *Full of protest, swearing thus . . .*

The Poet Queen paused, and then scratched out the words *swearing thus* and replacing them with *of oath*, and continued for another two lines.

> *As true as steel, as plantage to the moon,*
> *As iron to adamant, as earth to th' centre . . .*

The pen dropped. 'As though any patron would accept this codswallop!' the Poet Queen moaned bitterly, squinting and producing tears, though not because of the dimness of the room. It was the make-up. This mixture of powdered eggshell paste crumbled when it dried and flecked into the eyes, causing great stinging.

Leaning back in the chair, the Poet Queen cried, 'I cannot do this.'

'Is there a problem?' a light voice asked from somewhere in the room. The bent figure of Robert Cecil was spotted near a hunting tapestry with such a sense of stillness that at first he appeared to be a woven figure within it.

'I thought I was alone. I did not hear you enter.'

'You know as well as I that I am endowed not to be heard entering,' Cecil said, stepping toward the table and emerging into the flickering light.

Would that this man could somehow be persuaded to take on the role of Richard, Duke of Gloucester, the Poet Queen thought, surveying Cecil's small and slightly deformed frame. *He is the very image of the changeling I saw in my mind's eye while writing the character.* But as all of society knew, that was impossible. The very thought of a noble, let alone a courtier, gracing the stage of any of the wooden rings of Southwark was unthinkable. Almost as absurd as the notion that her majesty Elizabeth Regina was the one composing the plays performed in Southwark.

'Ah, I see,' Cecil said with a wry smile after glancing at the foolscap and ink on the table, 'we are still performing the role of the playwright.'

'It is exercise for my mind. You do wish me to have a clear mind, do you not, Robert?'

'Of course, of course. What new work is

this, if I may so ask?'

'*The Famous Historie of Troilus and Cressida.*'

'And another masterwork, I trust. As notable as *Twelfth Night?*'

'A damnable mess is what it is proving to be! If this goes on the boards we shall have to clear the street of horses in front of the Globe Playhouse, lest we provide the groundlings with ammunition.'

'Surely it cannot be as dreadful as that. You have rarely failed your audiences before.'

'I have rarely been as distracted as I am now. I assume that you are here to tell me it is time for the matter at hand.'

Cecil nodded. 'His Royal Highness James of Scotland and his court are already on their way to the palace.'

'And you are absolutely convinced that this is the fittest course to take?'

'I would not have ventured anything so daring were it not my belief in the absolutely necessity of it.'

'Very well.' The imposing white-faced figure rose slowly from the chair and then dug at the broad vibrantly red wig. 'This feels as though it is made of horsehair.'

'I am sorry. It is the new one.'

'This cannot be one of Mountjoy's.' Christopher Mountjoy was a Huguenot wigmaker of renown.

'Alas, there was no time to employ Mountjoy.'

'It will have to do. How do I look?'

'Every inch the Queen,' Cecil replied with an obsequious bow.

The wig slipped again. 'Would that your self-satisfaction was contagious.'

'I am always satisfied when that which needs to be done is accomplished in an efficient manner, no matter what it is that needs to be done.'

'Whatever needs to be done. Were you not chief minister to the Crown, Robert, you might make a superb executioner.'

'If my Queen wished it, and if I could but lift an axe above my head, I would be more than happy to comply. However, since I cannot physically wield any weapon larger than a dirk, I must continue to do what needs to be done using only my brain. At this moment, my brain is telling me that before we greet his majesty King James that we must eradicate the smudge of ink on the middle finger of your right hand, which identifies you as a scribe. It would neither be politic nor wise to proclaim to the King of Scots that England's sovereign majesty is also the leading light of our playhouses.'

'I give you my word that neither the King of the Scots, nor any other man, shall ever hear such an admission from my lips. The truth of Elizabeth Shakespeare Regina will remain our secret.'

'Of course. Now we must go.'

The two proceeded to the throne room of Richmond Palace, normally a hubbub of human activity, but on this evening all but deserted. This audience with the son of the woman whom Elizabeth had executed sixteen years previously was to be a private and secret one, too critical and politically dangerous to involve any other personages, which meant that the other courtiers, even the Queen's ladies in waiting, had been banished for the night.

'Do you need me to assist you to the throne?' Cecil asked.

'This dress is as stiff and unwieldy as a sedan chair, but I shall manage.'

'I will announce His Royal Highness when he arrives. May God guide you this evening, and I pray that your infirmities will not be too visible to his majesty,' Robert Cecil declared, bowing his crooked frame even lower as he backed out of the room and went to await the arrival of King James the Sixth of Scotland.

Now alone in the cold cavernous room, the figure on the throne re-examined all ten fingers to ensure that any trace of ink had been eradicated, and thought: *May God go with me indeed, and may what I am about to do strengthen, and not destroy, England; and may there not be one more death in the palace before the evening is out.*

Straightening out the folds of the voluminous dress, which had become miscomfrumpled as a result of being wedged into a plain chair at the writing desk, the Poet Queen whispered: 'By the grace of God I am Elizabeth Regina, the Queen of England and Ireland, and I will brook no challenges to my authority and dignity, not even from the King of the Scots.'

But God in Heaven, how this damnable wig itched!

1

Queen Anne Street, London
1906

For what was probably the fourth time in a quarter hour, I glanced up at the clock that continued to taunt me by confirming that time was all but standing still.

Closing my book, I rose from the chaise and moved to the front window, pulled back the curtain, and looked out into the street. The living of London paraded by: people walked about from a definite *here* to a more uncertain *there*; vendors announced their wares in braying voices; horse-drawn carriages clopped down the street in workaday fashion; packs of boys raced past gentlemen and genteel women alike, displaying the sort of youthful disdain for others that would mature into careers as either criminals or politicians; and one of those red smoking two-deck motorized omnibuses bullied its way through

the thoroughfare like a Trojan horse passing into the city not with a hidden cache
of warriors inside, but rather the threat of
a changing world.

Time still existed out there. It was only
here, in my home, that it appeared to stop.

'Oh, heavens, Amelia, stop feeling sorry
for yourself,' I said aloud, knowing that I
would be heard by no one else, because
no one else was here to listen. This was
my fifth day of solitude, though it seemed
more like a fortnight. I had been alone
before, of course; but this time, owing to
the absence of both my husband and my
maid, I felt abandoned.

For once, John's absence had nothing
to do with his strange and often annoying
friend Mr. Sherlock Holmes, who was, so
far as the world at large was concerned,
living in retirement. It was the other Holmes
brother, Mycroft, a high-ranking member
of His Majesty's government, who had
pulled John away from me this time, by
drafting him to serve as a delegate for the
International Conference for the Revision
of the Geneva Convention in Switzerland.
While this was far more John's province

than my own, I had at least learned that the objective was to establish provisions for the treatment of sick and wounded soldiers on the battlefield. Since John's dramatic recountings of his exploits with Sherlock Holmes, which appear regularly in popular magazines, had made him one of the world's most famous surgeons, and a former military man of near equal repute, he could hardly resist, particularly with the understanding that any official request from Mycroft Holmes was a *de facto* command from the King himself. As far as I was concerned, the best provision for the treatment of wounded soldiers was to prevent armed conflict and not wound them in the first place, but the Crown had not solicited my opinion.

The absence of Missy Trelawny, who had been in our employ for some four years now, over which time she had matured from a rather flighty girl to a slightly less flighty girl, required no such royal edict; John had simply requested that she accompany him to help him in his journey. Helping to saving damsels from living burial and dispatching deadly snakes before they could kill might be John's cup of tea, but preparing his own cup of tea each afternoon was, alas, not.

Standing in the middle of the silent, empty room, I decided that I was not about to spend the entire afternoon and evening here alone. Three can play at the game of absence as easily as two. Picking up the morning's copy of the *Times*, I paged through it until I came to the adverts for theatres and concert halls. Immediately my eye fell upon a notice for *Peter Pan*, which continued to play at the Duke of York's. I looked past it, since I had enough aging boys who wouldn't grow up in my life already. *The Scarlet Pimpernel* at the New Theatre remained the toast of the West End, but derring-do on stage held little attraction for me. Perhaps there was something in the way of a concert or recital that might provide some diversion for the evening.

It was then that I noticed a tiny advertisement for a lecture on Shakespeare being held this evening at Madame Tussaud's Wax Museum, of all places. The write-up gave very little indication of the specifics of the lecture, except to note that one of the world's leading Shakespearean scholars, Professor Todhunter Macnee, of Moosejaw College, from somewhere in the United States, would be delivering the remarks, which would be based on his years of research into the Bard of Avon. The fact that the man actually had the courage to stand up before an audience and admit that he represented a place called Moosejaw College alone merited attendance. Eight o'clock was the assigned hour for the lecture, which gave me far more than enough time to prepare myself, get dressed and even partake of supper out, should I so choose. That would be an act of decadence, would it not?

The evening was a pleasant one, and I enjoyed walking from past Manchester Square, but slowed my pace upon realizing that the most efficacious route to Madame Tussaud's and the lecture forced me to turn into Baker Street, and ultimately walk past number 221, the first floor of which had for years served as the home of my husband and Mr. Holmes. For a brief moment I contemplated knocking on the door to say hello to Martha Hudson, the delightful owner of the place, but then thought better of it. Mrs. Hudson would want to talk about nothing but John and Mr. Holmes and their years together, and I was rather hoping instead to have a crime-free evening.

Upon arriving at Madame Tussaud's, I saw that there were a few people milling about the entrance and a small sandwich sign had been set up which read: *Lecture This Evening*. I was delighted to discover that there was no charge for the event, and so followed the gathering of people into the foyer of the museum.

'Ladies and gentlemen, the lecture is about to commence. Please be so good as to follow me,' announced a man standing to the side of a distinguished-looking wax figure that I immediately recognized as Charles Dickens. (Heavens, I had imagined him taller!)

We were led to a medium-sized meeting room that had a small stage area in front, complete with teaser curtains hanging from the ceiling and a podium in the centre, and several rows of seats with an aisle down the middle. On one side of the stage, standing in what looked uncomfortably like an open coffin, was a wax figure of William Shakespeare — and at last I understood why the lecture was taking place here instead of any of the other lyceums that dotted the landscape of London. None of the others would have possessed such a figure. Why the effigy of Shakespeare was encased in a black box, however, was something I could not fathom. Perhaps it was protection against the lighting in the meeting room, which was brighter than the lighting in the museum itself. In any event, I took my seat and waited for the presentation to begin.

Its start was signalled by a dimming of the lights in the audience section, and the simultaneous rise of illumination on the placid and somewhat eerie wax figure. A few moments later, a tall man with unruly reddish hair strode out from the wings and stepped to the podium, toting a sheaf of papers. 'Good evening to you all,' he said in an oddly accented voice. 'I am Professor Todhunter Macnee, chair of English studies at Moosejaw College in

Snowshoe, Washington, in the United States of America. I am delighted to be here in London. If you have ever spent much time in Snowshoe, Washington, you would surely understand that.'

That line was delivered with a bit of nervousness and force, but it drew a few chuckles from the audience. Todhunter Macnee looked no more than forty years of age, if that, which was rather young to be a professor and a Shakespeare scholar; then again, the Americans were by nature an exigent people, so unlike those of us here in England. Our university dons seemed to be born elderly.

He went on: 'We are here this evening to talk about the premiere dramatic voice and supreme poet of the English language, Mr. William Shakespeare.' Then he paused and repeated the name dramatically: 'William Shakespeare. That is the name by which this genius has been called by history. It is not, however, the true name and identity of the poet.'

Oh, *heavens*! Was this to be one of those arguments that William Shakespeare, gentleman of Stratford-upon-Avon,

16

was not the true author of the plays, poems and sonnets? If so, that would put the lecturer's youth in a more understandable light: he had *not* spent a lifetime acquiring knowledge about the Bard; he was merely a revisionist. Had I known that this was to be the nature of the talk, I would have most certainly stayed away.

I was gratified to see that I was not the only one in the audience who felt thusly, as there were several other voices that immediately began grumbling, and even booing the lecturer. If it bothered the speaker, he did not show it, but merely smiled and went on.

'Please, ladies and gentlemen, I beg you, hear me out,' Professor Macnee said, and the grumbling did quiet down. 'You may be of the assumption that I am hoping to convince you that the author of such timeless theatrical works as *The Tragedy of King Lear, Hamlet, Macbeth* and *As You Like It*, as well as the poems 'The Rape of Lucrece' and 'Venus and Adonis', was a different man from the fellow from Stratford, whose father was a humble glove-maker, and who found his way to London to become a player on the stage. But you would be wrong, my friends. I am not here to argue that William Shakespeare was some other man.'

The grumbling voices abated a bit and people settled back in their seats.

'For the fact is,' Professor Macnee said, capitalizing on the proffered second chance, 'that William Shakespeare was not a man at all, but rather a *woman*.'

Unlike the previous random grumbling, the response to this bombshell was an empty, airless silence, followed in short order by a few cat-calls and laughter. My own response was somewhere in between the two. Professor Macnee greeted this reaction to his second provocative statement with the same smiling aplomb with which he had accepted the initial protestations. When the wave of derisive murmurs had begun to abate, he held his hand up calmly for silence.

'My friends, I ask a simple question: why is the thought that a woman could have composed the works of Shakespeare so impossible to consider? Are we saying that no woman in history has ever had the brains for it? There is absolutely no reason for accepting as an impossibility the idea that a woman could be the intellectual equal of a man . . . unless it is to ascribe to her intellectual superiority.'

Now he had my attention. In fact, I was beginning to develop a newfound respect for this rustically endearing American scholar. What a pity the students of Oxford, Cambridge or Eton could not be exposed to such theories!

'I put it to you thusly,' Professor Macnee went on. 'Can we really believe that the creation of a character such as Lady Macbeth was the work of a man? Could a male author really limn her with such incredible complexity with such a degree of femaleness? I say to you, no. A male writer, even a male writer of genius, would have instead turned her into a form of Grendel's mother, an inhuman monster without an ounce of woman-hood. And while she is perhaps not someone I would cheerfully invite over for afternoon tea — ' Here he paused for a smattering of laughter. ' — Lady Macbeth is not an inhuman monster. Our fascination with her, our fear of her, if you will, lies in her essential humanity. Her tragedy would not resonate so resoundingly were she simply a caricature.'

This drew a nod of agreement, or at least consideration, by a few in the audience.

'By the same token,' the professor continued, 'would the essential weakness that is characteristic of her husband come naturally to a male writer? Perhaps it would, though perhaps it would not. Perhaps it takes a feminine vision to truly see a weak man.'

Here Professor Macnee paused to take a sip of water from a glass that was stationed at his podium and shuffled through a few pages of notes, after which he began again.

'The question that naturally follows is, who was this mystery woman? Who of that era possessed the intellect, breeding, education and genius to offer the world the works that we recognize as those of William Shakespeare of Stratford? There is but one logical conclusion.'

With that, he turned to the figure of Shakespeare in the box on the stage and he gestured toward it, and the effigy of William Shakespeare began to fade and disappear! In its place, as though by magic, now stood the figure of a woman, clad in a full-skirted dress and jewelled bodice, and wearing a circular wig of bright red hair.

'I give you the true author of the works of William Shakespeare,' Professor Todhunter Macnee proclaimed. 'Her Royal Highness, Elizabeth Regina of England.'

2

The majority of the assemblage was standing in amazement, though it was impossible to tell whether they were reacting to the audacity of Professor Macnee's claim or the stunning effect of William Shakespeare turning into Elizabeth before their eyes. For me, that was the easiest part to fathom; the professor had used a form of stage illusion known for some reason as a pepper's ghost, which works with mirrors, two carefully placed objects, and light sources to create the impression that one object has turned into another. That would explain why the figure of Shakespeare appeared in a box, rather than standing freely on the stage, since the confines of a box were required to facilitate the proper lighting needed to pull the trick.

'Ladies and gentlemen,' Professor Macnee was calling, 'please, ladies and gentlemen, your eyes have not forsaken you. Nothing truly miraculous has occurred here, I assure you; simply a bit of stage illusion to prove a point. And to prove the point even more so, please watch carefully.'

As one, the members of the audience quieted and took their respective seats. Once calm had resumed, the figure of Queen Elizabeth began to shift once more; only now instead of turning completely into Shakespeare, the lighting change stopped halfway, revealing a cross between the two figures.

This proved to be the most startling demonstration of all, and the knowing smile on the face of Professor Macnee indicated that he clearly anticipated it being so; for while the bodies and hairstyles of the wax effigies were frozen in eerie translucence because of the lighting trick, their facial features remained solid and eerily identical.

The face of the Poet Queen hung eerily atop the blurred outlines of their respective bodies, an eerie sight that reduced each member of the audience to meek silence. 'I can guess what some of you are thinking,' Professor Macnee said evenly. 'You may be presuming that I simply had two identical figures made with the same mould and then costumed them differently. That would easily explain this resemblance, would it not? So let me assure you, ladies and gentlemen, that these are the figures of Will Shakespeare and Her Majesty the Queen that are normally on display here at Madame Tussaud's, having been created by this establishment's unequalled artists through the most painstaking of research. They have simply moved here for my specific purposes of presenting a startling visual metaphor. As for the illusion itself, it was arranged for me by an associate who is a well-known figure of the London theatre and eminently well versed in stagecraft, Mr. Hathaway Broughton, esquire. Come out and take a well-deserved bow, Mr. Broughton.'

From the side of the stage near the pepper's ghost illusion strode a figure dressed in a long black coat of the fashion favoured by the recently demised Sir Henry Irving and a high, stiff collar. A monocle covered his right eye, though the tilt of his head implied that only by looking up was it kept in place. Even standing as erect as a statue, the man was not tall (in fact, he barely came up to Professor Macnee's shoulder), and his face wore an expression of calm wisdom. I clasped my hand to my mouth to prevent myself from laughing out loud when I realized that Hathaway Broughton was really my old friend Harry Benbow.

After taking a grandiose bow, 'Broughton' looked out into the audience and caught my gaze straight on. After an almost imperceptible private bow to me, he turned on his heel and fled the stage.

As I was trying to recover from the surprise appearance by Harry, with whom I had acted years ago in an amateur theatrical troupe, but who had since proven to be something of a lightning rod for trouble, a man in the audience thrust up his hand and was recognized by Professor Macnee.

'Did not Queen Elizabeth die many years before Shakespeare?' the man asked. 'How do you explain that discrepancy?'

'Excellent question, sir, thank you. You are quite correct, Her Majesty Elizabeth Regina died thirteen years before Will Shakespeare of Stratford, and several years before the last Shakespearean plays were produced. But we all know that the author of the plays worked with collaborators, among them — '

Professor Macnee consulted his notes again before continuing.

' — John Fletcher, Thomas Middleton, perhaps Thomas Kyd. I do not want to leave anyone out.' He pronounced the word *out* as though it was a morsel eaten by a horse, in the manner of a Canadian national, but I supposed that Snowshoe, Washington must have been near enough to the Canadian border to share a dialect. 'That, however,' the professor went on, 'does not explain the Shakespeare half of the equation, does it? I submit that it is reasonable to suggest that Queen Elizabeth left a stockpile of stories, or even entire drafts of new works at the time of her death, which were revised or enhanced by others over the next several years.'

'All well and good,' another man called out, 'but this is nothing but theatrics. Where is your proof?'

'While I am not prepared to reveal it at present, I can tell you that I have discovered a letter written by a very high-level member of Her Majesty's court which I believe to be proof conclusive.'

A small white-haired man in the front row was the next to raise his hand.

'Yes sir, you have a question?'

Instead of trying to shout it out, the white-haired man rose and stepped toward the stage, motioning for the lecturer to lower himself in order to converse with him, which Professor Macnee did with a bemused expression on his face. Kneeling down on the apron of the stage, he bowed his head low so the old man could whisper into it. Then with a smile he rose and resumed his place behind the podium, while the white-haired spectator went back to his seat.

'The gentleman in front posed another excellent question, and a very pertinent one, which is, why the subterfuge? Why would Her Majesty Queen Elizabeth, in addition to all her other accomplishments, not wish to be known as the greatest poet of the English language? We shall never know for certain, of course, though we can speculate. I believe the answer lies in the difference that three hundred years have wrought upon Shakespeare's place in culture. Today we regard him as the greatest genius in the English language. In his own time, however, Shakespeare was an entertainer of the masses, headquartered south of the Thames, which was what we in the States call the wrong side of the tracks. Hard as it may be to accept today, some three hundred years ago a production of *Hamlet* was considered no less lofty than watching a bear be poked with sticks in a pit. I could understand where a divinely chosen sovereign, as Elizabeth was then considered, might not wish her seal attached to it.'

After taking another round of questions and promising that he would be offering more persuasive proof of this theory in the form of an upcoming book, Professor Macnee declared his talk finished. He received polite, if not exactly thunderous, applause, which he in turn directed to the still cross-faded figure of Queen Shakespeare, before striding off the stage. Those around me were filing out of the hall; I, however, stayed where I was, as did the elderly man from the front. Before long, however, he turned and exited the room, which left only me.

Professor Macnee re-emerged from the side, and appeared startled to see me remaining in my seat. 'Yes, madam, do you have a question for me?' he asked.

'Actually, Professor, I am here to see your assistant, the eminent man of the theatre.'

'Indeed?' Turning to the backstage area, the professor called: 'Mr. Broughton, you have a visitor.'

'Hathaway Broughton' strode back onto the small stage as formally as though he were here to receive a knighthood, and bowed stiffly to me. 'Ah, Lady Pettigrew, how lovely to see you again,' he said in a plummy upper-class accent, and it was all I could do to prevent myself from what we in the theatre call *corpsing*, which is breaking character to laugh at the antics of a fellow player. 'You must excuse me, dear lady, while I help the professor strike the illusion we have created, and then I shall be at your disposal.'

'I shall wait,' I said.

As the two men began to dismantle the coffin-like box, carefully removing the double-purposed glass that forms a mirror when light is reflected upon its surface in the proper way, two others dressed in work clothes entered the lecture hall and lifted the figure of Shakespeare, carrying him away, presumably to his usual display area. By the time they returned to similarly remove the wax effigy of the Queen, the pepper's ghost illusion had been totally broken down.

Once they had finished, the professor turned to Harry and said, 'How lucky I was to find you, sir. Thank you for assisting me in my presentation.'

'My distinct pleasure, my good man,' Harry said, shaking the professor's hand. His monocle dropped from his eye, however, when Professor Macnee produced a roll of banknotes and peeled a few off, offering them to him for services rendered.

'Oh really, dear fellow, I couldn't accept this,' Harry protested. 'Really, I couldn't, not in the slightest, not at all . . . oh very well, if you insist.' He took the notes and bowed to the professor. 'If you would excuse me now, my dear fellow, I must attend to my visitor, who has been ever so patient.'

'Of course, Mr. Broughton, and thank you again.'

Still in character, Harry strolled my way, bowed, and offered his arm to escort me out of the hall, which he did with all due haste. Once we were out of earshot of Professor Macnee, the little man leaped into the air and kicked his heels together. '*Gor*, ducks!' he said in a stage whisper that contained no trace of the high-born accent he had been using only moments before. 'You see what that bloke give me? Five quid! All that sausage just for settin' up a blinkin' ghost for 'im! Walk-*er*!'

Now I did laugh, for it was safe to do so.

'This calls for celebration, ducks!' Harry said. 'How about joining me for a spot of Jim Skinner somewhere? I'm 'arf-pear-halved.'

Those born within the sound of the Bow bells, as Harry had been, would know that *Jim Skinner* meant *dinner*, though *'arf-pear-halved* was new to me; I

31

could only surmise through the context that it meant *hungry*.

'I don't know, Harry. It is getting a bit late, and I should be getting home.'

'Gotta get back for the doc, eh?'

'Well, no, he's out as well, but — '

'Then there you 'ave it! You're free for the evenin', Amelia, so why not have a little step-out? An' for the first time, yours truly is buyin'!'

I suppose he was right. There was nothing I would be doing at home except listening to the silence. 'Oh, very well, *Hathaway*. Let's go.'

'That's the spirit, ducks! *Gor*, Amelia, there's times when I think you worry too much. It ain't like someone's gonna die, or something.'

3

After promising to take me anywhere I wanted, Harry instead cast his sights on a public house called The Earl of Winchester; hardly my idea of a fine dining establishment, though I chose not to argue and spoil Harry's gay mood. I had already taken a bit of supper before the lecture anyway, and was not particularly *'arf-pear-halved*.

'How was it you became associated with this Professor Macnee, Harry?' I asked once we had settled around a table in an upstairs dining area, which was thankfully free of the thunderhead of tobacco smoke that obscured the ceiling of the bar below.

'Fate, ducks,' he replied. 'Pure fate, it was. I was havin' me bit o' fish one night when I looked at the paper it was wrapped in, and I spied this advert what said someone was lookin' for an expert in all things theatrical. Well, *gor*, they might as well 'ave been saying, 'Send us Harry bloomin' Benbow on a platter!' So I convinces a chum of mine who's a rat-catcher at the Haymarket to slip into wardrobe and slide me a set o' duds what befits a toff. He did, and I presented meself as Hathaway Broughton, esquire, late of the Royal Strand Theatre.'

'Wasn't the Royal Strand Theatre torn down last year?'

'That's why I was late of it, Amelia. But *gor*, did you hear that gasp come up from the audience when ol' sweet Will turned into Her blooming Highness?' He was still laughing gleefully when a waitress, or perhaps a barmaid with a clean apron, came to take our order. I ordered a pork pie, more out of politeness than hunger, and a pot of coffee, while Harry treated himself to a Scotch egg, a plate of jellied eel, and a steak and kidney pie, accompanied by a pint of bitter.

'The transformation was indeed effective,' I said after the waitress had gone. 'I'm curious, though: do you really believe the professor's theory?'

'I'm no blinkin' scholar, you know that. Seems right silly to me, if you want to know the truth. But the prof, he told me he's got some sort of proof that ol' Lizzie was really writin' the plays. Seems like the old girl already had quite a bit on her plate without the job of providin' the Globe with scripts, but he was convinced.'

'Well, I for one think it is preposterous,' I replied. 'I will not believe it until I see the man's proof with my own eyes, and even then I shall remain sceptical.'

'I figgered you weren't about to swallow the prof's theory. In fact, I thought twice afore sendin' you that invite.'

'Invite? I didn't receive any missive from you, Harry. I came as a result of seeing an announcement for the lecture in the newspaper.'

'No foolin'? Blimey, I hope I didn't waste a postage stamp. You live in the same place, right?'

I confirmed that we did, adding: 'The last post of the day had not yet been delivered by the time I left home, so perhaps I shall find it waiting for me.'

'Well, my girl, the important thing is that you came. Though I should ask for a refund on the bloomin' stamp.'

When the food came, I nibbled and Harry devoured. This was likely more food than he had seen over the last week.

It was slightly after eleven o'clock when I rose to leave, my stomach aching not from the pie, but from the steady stream of Harry's jokes and antics. True to his word, Harry paid for our meal and then walked me outside, where he resumed his highborn persona to hail a cab for me, which he also paid for. 'I shall see you again soon, Harry,' I said through the opening of the hansom.

'You may count on it, milady,' he drawled, bowing deeply as the cab pulled away.

Upon returning home to Queen Anne Street, I found a small packet of envelopes in the post, one of which was indeed from Harry, confirming my suspicion that it had been relegated to the nine-half delivery. Opening it, I pulled out the note which read:

Amelia I hope you can come down and pop in at this lil swaray at Madam Tussaud's tonite at 8 cause I can promise you a lil razle dazle. I been working with this prof from the colonies on a trick and hes so happy with the results hes ready to name me in his will! What Im gonna do at the show will slay 'em for sure! Just ask for Hathaway Broughton esk. Har Har Harry.

A second envelope was addressed to John; it was from the publishing house of Cushing and Neville, who had been reissuing his stories in book form. Wondering if it might be a cheque, I took the liberty of opening it. Withdrawing the negotiable slip of paper from the inside, I read the amount, smiled, and said, 'I hope you are having a wonderful time, darling.' Then I walked to his writing desk and slipped the cheque and envelope into the top drawer.

The third envelope was a bigger surprise: a letter from another old friend, Beth Newington, yet another former member of the Laurence Delancey Amateur Theatrical Company, along with Harry and me. This evening was practically turning into a reunion. I had corresponded with Beth over the years, but not recently, knowing that she was preoccupied with her husband Robert's ongoing illness. Oh, heavens . . . I hope this missive was not notification of bad news. Braving the sealed envelope with a letter opener, I withdrew a single sheet, covered in familiar handwriting, and began to read:

Dear Amelia:

I am so sorry to bother you in this fashion, but I must beg your assistance. My sister Mary, who lives in Stratford-upon-Avon, has a problem.

Stratford-upon-Avon, I thought; the second theme of this evening, it would seem.

It is her husband Graham . . . he has disappeared!

Good heavens!

She has contacted me for help and advice, but as you know, I am tending to my Robert, who has been showing slow signs of improvement, but not so many that I could pack up and leave him on his own. I know that you have often worked with the police on criminal cases, and that Scotland Yard considers you something of an honorary member, so I am appealing to you for help. Could you please write to Mary and advise her on what to do?

The remainder of the letter consisted of an address for Mary Chelish in Stratford and profuse thanks for any help I could give, and apologies for asking. Knowing Beth as I did, I understood what an ordeal it was for her to beg for any kind of assistance. Of course I would help. What were friends for? While I could not remember ever making the claim that I was a member of the Yard, honorary or not, I had gleaned enough of the workings of the police department and their methods over the course of my marriage to John, and my acquaintance with Sherlock Holmes, to point the unfortunate Mrs. Chelish into a comforting direction.

Seating myself at John's desk, I took up a piece of paper and pen, dipping it in the inkwell, and then set out to compose an encouraging note to Mary Chelish. After five minutes, I sat back and reviewed what I had written:

Dear Mary Chelish:

Crumpling up the paper, I threw it in John's waste bin. Taking up a fresh one and starting a new, I found I was able to increase my wordage output, since after several minutes, this one now read:

My dear Mary Chelish:

'Oh, this is absurd,' I muttered, discarding that page as well, and replacing the uncooperative pen back in its holder.

It was midnight, and I was tired. I would figure out what to write to Mary Chelish tomorrow.

As I prepared for my solitary bed, the quietude of the house descended on me like a shroud. It must have had the same practical effect, too, since within minutes of crawling between the sheets I was dead to the world.

*   *   *

The next morning I rose with the sun. After preparing myself for another still and quiet day inside, I decided to rebel and go out for a pot of tea and a bite of breakfast. After all, the cheque now sitting in John's desk allowed me a little financial freedom. After pinning on my hat, I left the house to revel in the glorious noise of London; even the mechanical chugging of those monstrous omnibuses was today welcome to my ears (albeit only slightly).

I had barely made it to Wimpole Street when I heard the harsh voice of a news-vendor calling: 'Brutal murder of an American! Read about it in the *Telegram*!'

I cannot explain why a strange chill began to form in the pit of my stomach, but it did. Hastening to the news-stand, I bought a copy of the newspaper from the motley-clad vendor and asked about the murder.

41

'Not the sort of tale for a genteel lady, mum,' he replied. 'But it's right there, on page one.'

Skimming the story, I read that the police had responded to a distress call at a private hotel in Grafton Street and there found the body of a man, identified as *Professor Todhunter Macnee*! 'Good lord!' I cried.

'See, mum? Shocking is what it is.'

'Yes . . . shocking.'

I resumed reading, learning that Professor Macnee had been shot to death a mere hour after I had seen him alive at Madame Tussaud's! The account went onto explain that papers found in the professor's let room linked him with a man involved in the London theatre, whom the police were seeking for questioning . . . a man named *Hathaway Broughton*.

Oh, Harry! I thought desperately. *How do you do it?*

4

There was no question, of course, that Harry was innocent of any wrongdoing in the man's death, but neither was there any question that Harry Benbow was one of the most ill-fated people on earth. At least this time it was a fictional person that the police were looking for, and not Harry under his own name, though that meant I had to find him and warn him not to maintain his disguise. I engaged a hansom cab to take me to Harry's last known address, a house in Lambeth, not far from the Vauxhall Bridge. I prayed he still lived there.

Upon arriving there some twenty minutes later, another worry presented itself in the form of a dark figure in a greatcoat loitering about in front of it. It was a man, though I could not make out his face due to a high scarf and a bowler hat pulled low. He appeared to notice the hansom as we approached the kerb.

Immediately I knocked on the roof and called: 'Driver, go past the house and around the corner.'

'What for?'

'Because I want you to. Please do as I request.'

'It's your shilling.'

We pulled away and traversed the street before turning into a narrow lane, at which point I knocked again. 'Please stop here,' I instructed. 'I shall walk the rest of the way.'

'As you say, lady.'

I got out and paid the scowling brute (why was it that hansoms were invariably operated by the most unhandsome of people?), who then pulled away and disappeared around the next corner. Walking back to Harry's street, I crossed over in order to keep an eye on the shadowy stranger without him seeing me. His all-too-apparent attempt to disguise himself implied that he was not a policeman, since a member of the Metropolitan force would have no need to resort to such mysterious tactics.

I waited and watched. Several times the

man looked as though he were about to enter the building, only to reconsider and once again scan the foot traffic on the sidewalk and the wheeled traffic on the lane. I had nearly come to the point of seeking a policeman myself when the figure finally withdrew a watch from his pocket and checked it, then slowly moved down the street, looking back every so many steps before he finally disappeared from view. As soon as he was out of sight I rushed to the door of Harry's building and rang the bell, which in due time was answered by a middle-aged woman I knew only as Moll. 'Oh, 'tis you, Mrs. Whitsett,' she said, grinning broadly enough to reveal her four remaining teeth.

'Watson,' I corrected. 'Is Mr. Benbow in?'

'Should be. I hain't seen him go.' She invited me in and together we stepped to the door marked 'A', upon which she knocked loudly. 'Mr. Benbow, a visitor.' There was no reply, so she knocked again. Finally I stepped close and said through the door: 'Harry, it's Amelia. If you're there, please let me in.'

Immediately the sound of a latch being

disengaged was heard, and the door creaked open. 'Hello, ducks,' he said. 'What brings you here?'

'I need to speak with you,' I said.

'I'll be off, then,' Moll said. 'No funny stuff, you two.' She turned and shuffled away.

'Can I come in?'

'Right,' Harry said, opening the door just widely enough to permit entry into the dark curtained room. 'I'm glad you're here, Amelia. Did you see him?'

'If you mean the man in the scarf and hat who was lurking out front, yes, I saw him. I don't believe he saw me, though.'

'That bloke's been out there the whole day, looking up at me from the street, like he knew I was here! As soon as he caught sight of me looking back, he spun around and pretended like he wasn't looking.'

'You have no idea who he is?'

'Not a bit. But his being there is giving me the willies, I can tell you that. Who'd be wantin' to spy on ol' Harry?'

'Have you seen a newspaper today?'

He shook his head. 'Haven't had me fish yet.'

I filled Harry in on the tragedy

involving Todhunter Macnee, stopping only to accommodate his repeated cries of '*Gor!*' By the time I was finished he looked pale. 'I don't get it, Amelia. Why's it always happen to me?'

'I don't know, Harry, but we would do better to focus instead on the immediate problem, which is that man outside. I have to get you away from here until we can get this entire matter settled.'

'Where would I go?'

'You can stay with me at Queen Anne Street,' I said.

'Blimey, that's a little cosy, ain't it? What'll the doc say to that?'

'Actually, he's on the continent until further notice.'

'Well, what about your maid, then? Won't she think it's a bit p'culiar?'

'She is with John.'

Harry's eyebrows shot up.

'Oh, really, Harry!' I said. 'It's nothing like that! It would take too long to explain what exactly it is, but my point is that I have the space for a while, and you need to get out of here. The problem is getting you past that strange man outside.'

'*Gor*, that's no problem,' Harry said, a sly smile colouring his face. He dashed over to a large, very worn and beaten steamer trunk and opened it, pulling out what appeared at first to be a small animal. Only upon closer inspection was I able to recognize it as a false beard. Harry opened a few other drawers in the trunk, pulling out some jars and sticks of makeup, and within minutes my friend had all but disappeared, replaced by an elderly, hirsute, bent man who looked like he could have been Gladstone's grandfather.

We hastened out of the building and down to the street, seeing no trace of the strange scarved figure. I spotted a cabriolet for hire at the end of the street and waved to him. While he pulled to the kerb, I went back in and got Harry, who hobbled to the street as though he were a thousand years old. Raising a leg to step into the carriage, he faltered and then let it drop again. 'Please, Harry,' I hissed, 'just get in. We are attempting to avoid an audience, not attract one.'

'Sorry, ducks,' he whispered back, and then hopped into the cab.

'If you happen to run into any of my neighbours, Harry,' I said, 'you are my cousin. All right?'

We spent the rest of the journey back to Queen Anne Street in silence, after which I paid the cabman and ushered Harry inside. '*Gor*, this'll be like living at the Ritz!' he said happily. Once he had removed his disguise and cleaned up, I sat down to think about what to do next. Harry was safe for the moment, but he could not stay here indefinitely. I did not share Sherlock Holmes's base opinion of the intelligence and abilities of the Metropolitan Police force; they would link Hathaway Broughton to Harry eventually. The simplest solution seemed to be to have Harry voluntarily go to the police and explain to them everything he knew about the professor. But when I proposed that to him, Harry turned uncharacteristically glum.

'You know, Amelia, that hasn't exactly worked in the past,' he said. 'Remember when the peelers accused me o' abdicatin' those two little tykes?'

'*Abducting*, Harry; and yes, I remember.'

'If it weren't for your dealin' with them

on my behalf, I'd be in the clink.'

I suddenly sat up. 'That's the answer, then. What if I were to visit Scotland Yard headquarters on your behalf? I am certain I could learn what papers the professor had that linked you — or at least Broughton — to him. I could also find out who is in charge of the case and speak to them. With any luck at all it will be my friend Inspector Laurie. If need be, however, I could try to see Melville Macnaghten himself.' Melville Macnaghten was the head of CID and a man with whom John and I had worked on more than one occasion.

'Think that'd do it?' Harry asked.

'It cannot hurt. The sooner this problem is cleared up, the better. You stay here, Harry, and I will pay a visit to the Yard.'

'What'll I do while you're gone?'

'If you are to be living at the Ritz, you should avail yourself of all the amenities, including a lovely bathtub in that room over there.'

'*Gor*, Amelia — '

'Not a word, Harry. Leave your clothes on the floor and I will find others for you, somehow.' Since the closest of anyone in the house to Harry's size was Missy, I looked in her bedroom for a nightgown, walked back out, and handed it to Harry.

'Gor, Amelia!' he shouted. 'You want me to dress like Ophelia?'

'It's only temporary, and I'll think of something better. Now draw the water and start scrubbing. I will be back.'

Ordinarily, I might be concerned about running up so many cab fares in one day, but the cheque from John's publisher remained fresh in my mind. After this one dropped me off in front of New Scotland Yard, I strode into the premises and told the officer at the desk that I was here to see Inspector Robert Laurie. Before he could do or say anything about it, I marched past and disappeared up the staircase. I knew exactly where the inspector's office was and went straight there. Rapping lightly on his door, I said, 'Hello, Inspector.'

Inspector Laurie looked up from his desk and smiled. 'My word, Mrs. Watson. How are you?' His voice carried a slight Scottish burr. He rose and approached me, taking me by the hand and escorting me in. 'I was not expecting you today, was I?'

'No, this is something of an impulsive visit. I read in the newspaper about that poor American college professor who was found murdered and I was compelled to come in.'

'You mean the Macnee case?' His normally sober face grew even more so. 'Terrible business. I've been briefed about that one, but I am not in charge of it. What exactly is your interest?'

I explained that I had been at the professor's lecture last evening and, since I was therefore among the last people to have seen him alive, I wanted to offer any help that I could as to his nature and character.

'Can't keep out of the action, eh?' he asked, with a wry half-grin. 'As I said, it is not my case. Inspector Islington is the man in charge of this one.'

'I don't believe I've met him,' I said.

A rare, fleeting half-smile appeared on his face, and Inspector Laurie stepped past me and swung shut the door to his office, as though fearful of being over-heard. 'Horrie Islington does not lead many investigations, though he has been on the force longer than any of us. In fact, some say that he was among the first recruits when Robert Peel formed it, eighty years ago.'

'Oh dear.'

'Don't get me wrong, Mrs. Watson. He's a good man, or was, in his prime. These days he takes charge of special cases that for one reason or other require a degree of sensitivity.'

'And the death of the professor is such a case?'

'Macnee was an American; and when a foreign national is murdered on English soil, it is not simply a police matter, but one for the Home Office as well. Therefore the chief commissioner has instituted a policy mandating that all such investigations be handled with a high level of discretion and tact. No one at the Yard can rival Islington for tact, to the point of obsequy. Let me take you down to his office.'

Inspector Laurie led me through the hallways of New Scotland Yard to a corner office that seemed as far away from the others as could be possible and knocked on the door. 'Come in,' a light voice answered from within, and we did.

Inspector Horatio Islington was large and a bit doughy, with wispy yellow-white hair combed rather desperately over his skull in an attempt to disguise its obvious thinness. Beneath these colourless strands, his face was incongruously childlike: smooth and unwrinkled with large wondering eyes and a bemused look that appeared to be less an expression than the natural cast of his features. Upon seeing me he rose to his full, considerable height and said, 'Ahhh Robbie, can this lovely young lady be your daughter?'

I confess that I was rendered a bit nonplussed by the flattery, despite the fact that Inspector Laurie had warned me of the man's penchant for fawning.

'Horrie, this is Mrs. Amelia Watson, who is a friend of ours. You may have heard of her husband, Dr. — '

'John H. Watson,' Inspector Islington finished, holding out a hand to me. 'Of course; I have read and enjoyed all of his works. Were he not such a gifted practitioner of the pen, he might make a fine detective himself.'

'I will tell him you said so,' I replied.

'Mrs. Watson is here about the Macnee case. She saw the victim the evening before he died.'

'Indeed? Sit down please, madam.'

'Thank you,' I said, taking a chair as Inspector Laurie excused himself and left the room. Inspector Islington meanwhile seated himself, leaning backwards in the chair and locking the fingers of his hands behind his head. 'Now then, what can you tell me about the unfortunate Professor Macnee?'

'Well, I attended his talk about Shakespeare at Madam Tussaud's, so it was such a shock to read of his death so soon afterward.'

'I see. Anything else?'

'Such as . . . ?'

'Such as the time you last saw him, perhaps?'

'Oh, it was after the talk had ended, around quarter past nine.'

'How observant you are, dear lady,' the inspector gushed. 'Was the professor still in the museum at the time you left?'

'Yes.'

'And do you happen to remember seeing a fellow by the name of Hathaway Broughton?'

Step cautiously, I admonished myself. 'Hathaway ... Broughton,' I repeated. 'Oh, yes, the man who assisted the professor with the lighting and such.'

'Quite. Did anything about him strike you as peculiar?'

'Peculiar? In what way?'

'In any way at all.'

'I cannot say that it did.'

'I see.' He rose and once more extended his hand. 'Thank you so much for coming in, Mrs. Watson. Please do give my best regards to your husband.'

'I shall,' I replied, taking his hand, surprised by his sudden dismissal. 'If you do not mind my asking, though, I am curious as to why you think there was something peculiar about Mr. Broughton.'

'In my experience, dear lady, all criminals betray a signature peculiarity, each in his or her own way.'

'Criminals?'

'Oh yes, particularly murderers.'

'Then you believe that Hathaway Broughton — '

'Is as guilty of the murder of Todhunter Macnee as the days are long in June,' Inspector Islington said cheerfully.

5

It took all of my skill as a former actress to keep the look of horror from registering on my face. 'I marvel at the speed at which you have solved the case,' I said, my mouth dry as dust.

'Oh, we have not made an arrest, but it is only a matter of time,' Inspector Islington replied. 'First we must discover the chap's real name.'

'Real name?'

'Oh, yes, just so. You see, this fellow who called himself Broughton was working with the unfortunate Professor Macnee clearly to gain his trust and thus take advantage of him. Robbery, I believe, was the motive, since the constable who first arrived at Professor Macnee's hotel room saw that the place had been ransacked. Upon inspection, a piece of paper was uncovered, and on it was written the name Hathaway Broughton, with the appellation 'actor/manager', and stating his affiliation with the Royal Strand Theatre.'

'I see. But how does that tell you that the man was using an assumed name?'

'Because our men have spent the last several hours speaking with anyone we could find who is connected to the London stage, and no one has ever heard of a Hathaway Broughton. Furthermore, the Royal Strand Theatre is no longer in operation. Why, you may ask, being a clever woman, would a man decide to present himself under an alias, and with a falsified history? Because he does not want to be detected. Why does he not want to be detected? Because he is setting up a crime. Were it me who was planning to murder someone, I would not do so under my real name either. No, my dear Mrs. Watson, this case is unusual in my experience in that its solution seems so self-evident.'

I desperately wanted to counter his deduction with the fact that Harry could not possibly have been the killer, since no one of Harry's diminutive size could have overcome so large a man as Professor Macnee; but to do so would be to admit that I knew Harry, or 'Hathaway', better than I was letting on. Instead, I tried a different approach. 'I only hope you take care when apprehending this Broughton brute.'

'We always perform our task with care, dear lady.'

'Of course. But what I meant was that the professor looked to be a very sturdy and robust American, and any man who could physically get the better of him must be dangerously strong.'

The inspector smiled inscrutably. 'Please do not take this the wrong way, madam, but I believe that, given the chance, *you* could have physically gotten the better of Professor Macnee.'

'I? Inspector, I am not certain I care for that remark. I realize that I am tall for a woman, but — '

In an instant, and with surprising agility, he was around the desk and facing me directly, literally patting my hand. 'Oh, my dear Mrs. Watson, I apologize profusely if you took any negative inference from my comment,' he said. 'I was casting no aspersion on your delicacy, I assure you. It is simply that our victim was small and rather old, and had an artificial leg. A fellow like that would be very hard pressed to put up resistance.'

I stared back dumbly. 'Old?' I asked. 'Small?'

'Of course. You saw the man yourself, did you not?'

'Oh, oh yes. I supposed he seemed . . . younger and more robust on stage.'

'The illusion of the theatre,' the inspector chuckled. 'No, our unfortunate Todhunter Macnee was seventy-one years of age, as attested to by both his white hair and the identifying papers found on his body.'

With utmost politeness, Inspector Islington thanked me again for coming in and then ushered me out of his office. There was no longer any reason for me to remain at Scotland Yard; quite the opposite, in fact, for I now had to return home to inform Harry that he was in even deeper trouble than I had initially feared. On the way out of the building, one question launched an assault upon my mind: if Professor Todhunter Macnee was small, elderly and weak, who was the man I saw delivering the lecture?

Once I was out on the street, my mind cleared sufficiently well to remember that I had promised to find Harry a new suit of clothing. After hailing yet another cab, I gave the driver an address in Marylebone, that of John's favourite clothier. Harry's usual wardrobe announced itself as working-class, while the suit that he had worn as Hathaway Broughton reeked of Mayfair. Something in between was required.

Once we had arrived at the clothier's, I dashed in, hoping I would not be recognized by the proprietor, Mr. Rothstein. Alas, I was.

'How are you, Mrs. Watson?' he asked. 'And how is the good doctor? Something in the way of a waistcoat for him today, perhaps?'

'Um, no, actually, I am not shopping for him,' I said. 'I need a complete suit for . . . uh . . . my nephew.'

'I see. What size is the young gentleman?'

As best I could I described Harry, and when I was finished, Mr. Rothstein's eyes lit up. 'Madam, you are in luck,' he said, disappearing into the back room and returning a few moments later holding a beautiful pearl-grey suit with a matching waistcoat in roughly the same size. 'This was returned by a family whose lad had outgrown it even before I could finish it,' he said. 'I can give it to you at a greatly reduced price.'

He was as good as his word, and I was more than happy to take the suit off his hands, along with a linen shirt, a necktie, two pairs of stockings, and an undergarment. After carefully wrapping them in paper and string, the clothier handed them over to me with a smile. I opened my purse to pay him, but realized that I was not carrying enough money. The parade of cabs had finally caught up with my finances.

'Shall I send you a bill, then?' Mr. Rothstein asked.

'Yes, please do, thank you so much.' I took the items and left, hoping that when the bill arrived, I would be the one to open it, and not John.

After returning home, I was pleased to find Harry with damp hair and clad in the nightgown I had left for him — pleased, but also amused.

'I shall send your clothes out for cleaning,' I told Harry.

'Great, ducks. But I can't really toddle around in this all day, can I?'

'Of course not.'

I handed him the packages, which he opened cautiously, as though he was expecting a complete lady's evening gown. When he saw the contents, his face turned into that of Tiny Tim's on Christmas morning.

'*Gor*, ducks, you've done the impossible,' he said. 'You've rendered ol' Harry speechless.'

'Go into the bedroom there and try them on,' I said, pointing out Missy's room.

While he was in the other room, I scooped up his old clothing and carried it to the hamper. Harry soon emerged from the bedroom, resplendent in his new suit. My judgments of Harry's sizes proved to be largely accurate: the shirt fit fine, the trousers of the suit were only slightly large around the waist, and the waistcoat hung a bit, but the jacket looked as though it had been tailored specifically for him. 'Gor, Amelia, I don't even look like meself no more!'

'That is the idea. Sit down, Harry. I'm afraid I have some bad news.' I began informing him of the situation regarding Professor Macnee's death, the fact that he had been working for an imposter, and Inspector Islington's suspicions. As I did, his face fell into such a naked state of shock that I was immediately convinced he knew nothing about any part of it. Even Harry was not that good an actor.

'Crikey, how could that bloke have been a faker?' he cried.

'How is not impossible to explain,' I replied. 'He introduced himself as Macnee, spoke with a North American accent, and none of us were any the wiser. The real question is why.'

'It's all a hugger-mugger to me. Gor, ducks, you don't think it was the fake 'un what killed the real 'un, do you?'

'I don't know what to think. All I can state with any degree of certainty is that I failed completely in my objective, which was to find a way for you to go in to speak with the police and remove the suspicion from yourself. As far as the inspector in charge of the case is concerned, you are the prime suspect. Rather, Hathaway Broughton is.'

'Don't hardly matter, 'cause he's me. Blimey, ain't there someone else in the city who can be a prime suspect, just for once?'

'We will find a way to prove your innocence, Harry, don't worry.' He did not have to worry; I was doing enough for the both of us.

After watching Harry pace back and forth in the living room like a caged animal for a half hour, I finally said, 'For heaven's sake, Harry, please sit down.'

'I can't, Amelia. I'm too nervous.' Instead he went to the window that looked down onto the street. 'Crikey, I think someone's watchin' again!' he said.

'Is it the man in the scarf?' I asked.

'Nope, a different bloke this time.'

Rushing to the window, I saw a figure walking lugubriously in front of our house. He stopped, pulled out a slip of paper, examined it, and then looked up at the door. 'Oh, no!' I cried. 'That is Inspector Islington, the man in charge of the murder case! He appears to be coming in!'

'What's he want?'

'I have no idea. We'll have to hide you somewhere, but where? We do not have much concealed space in this house.'

'Has the doc got a mac?'

I knew what Harry was thinking, having seen him perform this trick before. 'In the closet by the front door,' I told him, and he dashed over to it, disappearing inside, just as I heard the doorbell ring. Answering it, I feigned surprise. 'Inspector, good heavens, what brings you to my home?' I asked.

'And such a lovely home it is, on such a beautiful street,' he fawned. 'I obtained your address from Robbie Laurie. I hope I have not overstepped my bounds in doing so.'

Actually, what he overstepped was our threshold, so he was now inside our house without actually being invited by me. 'I am surprised, is all,' I said, moving back to allow him greater ingress. 'What can I do for you?'

'Is there a more comfortable place in which we can converse?'

'Of course. Follow me, please.' I led him into the day room, which he appeared to savour as though visiting a foreign museum.

'May I congratulate you on your taste in décor and furnishing, Mrs. Watson,' he said.

'Thank you. Now, what is the purpose of your visit?'

'Well, madam, the most astounding thing happened after you paid your visit to my office this morning. I could not help noticing that you appeared somewhat uncertain in regards to my description of the late Professor Macnee. The fact that so observant a personage as yourself should react in such a way prompted me to dispatch one of my men back to Madame Tussaud's with a photo of the man. What do you suppose he found out?'

'I've no idea.'

'That the man claiming to be the professor was someone else entirely. He was described to me as tall, no more than middle-aged, and with reddish hair; quite unlike our Todhunter Macnee, but consistent with your recollection of his being young and robust.'

'Yes, well, that would explain things, wouldn't it?'

'Some things, yes, quite,' the inspector agreed affably. 'Unfortunately, there are many other matters to this case that remain conundrums, such as who the ersatz scholar really was.'

'I am afraid I cannot help you there.'

'Oh, I am quite convinced of that, Mrs. Watson, for if you did know anything about either imposter, you no doubt would have told me by now, wouldn't you?'

'Of course,' I prevaricated out of necessity.

'Of course,' Inspector Islington echoed, and then he began looking around the room as though searching for something. I confess I was becoming rather more annoyed by his manner and insinuations than fearful of his presence.

'Would you like to search the premises?' I enquired.

'Oh, dear lady, why on earth would I

wish to do that?'

'I'm sure I do not know, but clearly you are in search of something, so if it would satisfy you, then by all means, search. Why not start with the closet, Inspector? Is not that where criminals hide in dramatic thrillers?' I threw the closet door open for him to inspect. It was filled with garments, galoshes, umbrellas, and the odd box or two. There was no trace of Harry Benbow, or anyone else, inside. 'Where next, Inspector? Under the bed, perhaps?'

'Madam, you cut me to the quick,' Inspector Islington said, wringing his hands and bowing in a manner that might have shamed Uriah Heep. 'You seem to believe that I am in some way prying.'

'Well?'

'Perhaps I have overstayed my welcome, for which I am most terribly sorry. I simply wanted to make absolutely certain that I had all of the facts correct, since you were so good as to travel out of your way to see me earlier.' He turned and headed for the door, but stopped when he got to the small table upon which rested the post. He began pawing through the letters.

'Is there something in my mail that interests you?' I asked.

'Oh, no, no, you have been most helpful, and thank you, thank you, Mrs. Watson. I shall take my leave now. Good day, dear lady. I shall show myself out.'

I dashed to the window and stood there until I saw him emerge onto the street below. Then I ran back to the closet. 'Harry,' I said, 'he's gone.'

From under my husband's greatcoat I saw two legs appear, and then Harry emerged fully from it. His trick of crawling inside a hanging garment to hide was not a difficult one, given his size. '*Gor*, ducks,' Harry said, 'I could feel his eyes on me even through the coat, like he somehow knew I was there.'

'I couldn't see you, and I *did* know you were there, Harry. But I know what you were feeling. The man has a way of looking at things, even furniture, as though he was assessing their guilt. I even caught him going through the mail . . . oh, oh *no*!'

'What's wrong?'

'That invitation you sent me was on top of the stack! The inspector had to have seen it!' I held it out to Harry and he scanned it, blanching when he came to the last line: *Just ask for Hathaway Broughton esk. Har Har Harry.* 'Dear lord,' I moaned, 'this means there is no way he cannot know that we are connected!'

'Blimey.'

I dropped the note back down on the stack on top of Mary Chelish's letter. That was when the solution came to me. Or if not exactly a solution, at least a way to gain time. 'Harry, I know what we're going to do,' I said.

'Line up a nice firing squad for me?' he replied dejectedly.

'No, we're going to go on a trip.'

'A trip, ducks?'

'Yes, one that will prove quite fitting.'

'You've lost me, luv.'

'It was Shakespeare that first brought us together years ago, through the Laurence Delancey Players,' I said, 'and it was because of Shakespeare that we are in this current mess. So why not go to

Shakespeare himself?'

Harry shook his head in puzzlement. 'How're we gonna do that?'

'By travelling to Stratford-upon-Avon, of course.'

It took little time for me to pack for the trip, though for Harry, packing was redundant; he was wearing everything he owned that was in fine enough shape to wear, except for his worn-out battered boots, which stood out dramatically against his new suit of clothes. From my husband's wardrobe I borrowed a spare pair of shoes he rarely wore anymore, which fit Harry remarkably well. For such a small man, he had large feet.

The bigger problem was money. We would require inn or hotel rooms in Stratford, and my purse at present was nearly as empty as the old woman's proverbial cupboard. There seemed to be only one solution: I would have to take John's cheque to the bank, deposit it, and withdraw the necessary funds for our flight. I hoped that there would not be a problem.

Leaving Harry behind once again, albeit dressed this time, I used the last of my available money to hire a cab to take me to the bank, knowing that if I failed in my task, we were not only not going to Stratford, but I was walking back home. To my great relief, the bank clerk saw the name 'John H. Watson' and was more than happy to comply with my wishes, writing 'For deposit into account' on the back in his own hand, and having me initial it. I left the bank with forty pounds, vowing to return to our account whatever I did not use during this escapade.

Roughly an hour and a half after my return to Queen Anne Street, Harry and I were seated in a comfortable second-class compartment on a train about to pull out of Euston Station for Stratford-upon-Avon. 'I can't believe you'd go to all this trouble, jus' for me, Amelia,' Harry said.

'Trouble is indeed the word, Harry,' I responded. 'Besides, I have other business to attend to while in Stratford.'

'Oh? What kind o' business?'

'I need to see someone. You remember Beth Newington, don't you? From the Delancey Players?'

'Beth Newington?'

'Wait, of course you don't. That's her married name. Back then she was Elizabeth Woodbine.'

'*Gor!* Little Lizzie Woodbine! Course I remember her! She's who's in Stratford?'

'No, her sister. Someone I've never met.'

'That's you, ain't it, ducks? Always willin' to help people out, even those what you never met.'

I could only hope that I would indeed end up helping everybody through the actions I was taking, myself included.

In another half hour we were out of the city and coursing through a pastoral landscape. 'Blimey, look at that, wouldja?' Harry said, peering through the compartment window. 'Just like a paintin', it is. With a sight like that, you feel nothing can really go wrong.'

The sudden sound of the compartment door being opened, and the man who stepped inside, belied that quite effectively.

'*Gor!*' Harry cried, recognizing the man. I recognized him as well. At least I recognized the bowler hat and the scarf that covered the brute's face.

6

Our visitor closed the compartment door behind him as both Harry and I shrunk back in our seats. Then he lowered the scarf and removed his hat.

'Good lord!' I cried as I looked into the face of the man who had given the lecture that night at Madame Tussaud's; the red-headed man Harry and I knew as Professor Todhunter Macnee.

'What do you want with us?' I demanded. 'Who are you?'

'Lady Pettigrew, isn't it?' the man asked, and I opted not to correct him, at least for the time being. 'Do not be alarmed, madam. I mean you no harm.' Reaching to the window, he slid the curtains closed and then seated himself next to Harry. 'I'm not much used to disguises,' he said, 'but since Mr. Broughton had seen my face, it was a necessity in order to remain anonymous.'

'Sir, I reiterate my questions,' I said.

'Who are you and what do you want with us?'

'My name is Gordon Plummer,' he replied, 'formerly of the Royal Canadian Mounted Police. Lately I've been living just below the border in the United States and working on my own as a private detective. Where are we going, by the way?'

'You don't know?' I asked.

'I followed the two of you onto the train. I am unaware of its destination.'

'Stratford-upon-Avon,' Harry offered.

'Really? We have a Stratford of our own in Ontario.'

'That's fascinating, Mr. Plummer,' I said, 'but would you be so good as to tell us exactly what this is all about?'

'Only if you promise to relax, Lady Pettigrew. I assure you, I mean you no harm. If you need further proof of that, here.' He reached into his pocket and pulled out a small revolver, the sight of which made Harry gasp. Then he handed it to me. 'Would I do that if I meant you any harm?'

'It might not be loaded.'

'Oh, it is, but I am confident you will

find no reason to use it. I offer it to you as proof that I am not a threat to you.'

'I dislike firearms,' I said.

'Lay it on the seat beside you, then.'

I did so.

'Now, as to why I am here. I was engaged by Professor Macnee to help him with a problem. You already know of his theory that Queen Elizabeth was Shakespeare. He had written some academic articles presenting this theory and was working on a book about it. He had also given a couple of lectures about it and as a result a handful of newspapers contacted him for interviews, and that's when the trouble started.'

'What trouble?' I asked.

'As word about the theory got out, he began to get letters in response. Most called him a nut or a crackpot, and those the professor laughed at. He said he could afford to, since he had proof of his convictions, which would someday be accepted as fact. But some of the letters were more disturbing. They appeared to come from the same source, and they contained threats.'

'What sort of threats?'

Before he could answer, a knock came to the compartment door, followed by the word: 'Conductor.' Mr. Plummer rose and opened it, revealing a uniformed man with a face like a melted candle. 'Tickets, please,' he drawled, for probably the hundredth time this hour. I passed Harry's and mine to the conductor, but since Mr. Plummer had neglected to purchase one before leaping onto the train, he was forced to settle up with the man on the spot. When the conductor had moved on, Mr. Plummer closed the door again and sat back down.

'So, where was I?' he muttered. 'Oh, yes. Initially the letters threatened him with public ridicule if he made his theory known, but later ones took a more serious turn. They began to threaten his life.'

'Oh dear. Who sent them to him?'

'That we do not know,' Mr. Plummer said. 'There was never a return address on them, but each carried a London postmark. Professor Macnee became concerned enough to seek help. He tried going to the police, but they treated the letters as jokes, so he sought out a private investigator and found me. Since it appeared that the person threatening him was never going to reveal himself, I came up with a plan to try and force him into the open. I convinced the professor that he should schedule a lecture in London, figuring that his nemesis would be compelled to show up and challenge him. It was a way of flushing the man out, like a game bird out of a bush.'

'Is that why you posed as the professor? To try and protect him?'

'Yes. Should some lunatic lunge at me from the audience, or brandish a weapon, I was more in a position to defend myself and even restrain the assailant than Professor Macnee, who was older and somewhat incapacitated due to age and a wooden leg. So the professor coached me on what to say and even tried to anticipate questions from the audience, in order to prepare the answers for me. He was there that night and cued me from the audience whenever I started to stray from the script.'

I now realized that the smallish

white-haired man in the front row who had asked pertinent questions matched the police description of Professor Todhunter Macnee exactly.

'Physical incapacity or not,' Mr. Plummer went on, 'once we arrived at Madame Tussaud's, and the professor saw the uncanny facial resemblance between the figures of Shakespeare and Queen Elizabeth, he practically began somersaulting. He was so excited over it. It was his idea to use the stage ghost effect to demonstrate the resemblance, but he did not know how to execute it, which is why we advertised for a theatrical expert — and found you, Mr. Broughton.'

'You certainly fooled me right well and good.'

'Yes, and I'm sorry about that, but it was necessary. Unfortunately, our subterfuge did not work. I think we flushed our man out all right, but instead of giving himself away, he remained hidden and later killed Professor Macnee.'

'Why have you been keeping watch on Harry, Mr. Plummer?' I asked.

'Harry? You mean Mr. Broughton?'

'Oh yes, I mean Mr. Broughton,' I said quickly. 'Harry is the name by which I call him.'

'To be honest, Lady Pettigrew, you and Mr. Broughton are the only leads I have in tracking Professor Macnee's murderer. You were at the lecture, and Mr. Broughton here worked directly with me on it. I suppose I should confess that I haven't been working as a detective for very long. In fact, this is my first case. I'm still trying to figure things out.'

'I see,' I said. 'Well, the two of us have confessions to make, too, and this seems as good a time as any to make them.'

The Canadian looked startled. 'You're confessing to the murder?'

'Of course not! I am admitting to equal subterfuge. You see, you are not the only poseur here. I am not Lady Pettigrew, though Pettigrew is my maiden name; and while Harry is indeed a man of the theatre, his name is not Hathaway Broughton. This is Harry Benbow and I am Mrs. Amelia Watson.'

'The wife of Dr. John Watson,' Harry added, but the red-haired man gazed back uncomprehendingly. 'You know, Sherlock Holmes? *That* Dr. Watson?'

'Sherlock Holmes?' Mr. Plummer said. 'He's a real person? I thought he was just a character in books.'

Harry and I exchanged glances, and then I turned back to the man across from me. 'My good sir,' I said, 'you may not be Todhunter Macnee, I may not be Lady Pettigrew, Harry may not be Hathaway Broughton, but I promise you, Sherlock Holmes *is* Sherlock Holmes.'

'Sorry,' he said, his face beginning to turn the colour of his hair. After an awkward pause, he changed the subject. 'So why are you going to Stratford?'

'Personal business,' I said. 'The sister of a close friend of mine lives there. She is experiencing a problem, and . . . well, Mr. Plummer, it is really nothing with which you should concern yourself. Suffice it to say that I am en route, and I have asked Harry to join me because . . . well — '

'So I could stay one step ahead o' the peelers, who seem to think that I kilt the ol' boy,' he blurted out.

'Oh,' Mr. Plummer said, and the only

sound in the compartment for the next minute was that of the train wheels clacking on the rails, after which the Canadian cleared his throat and said, 'Would you think me rude if I asked if either of you were the ones who sent that threatening mail to Professor Macnee?'

'Yes I would think you rude,' I replied, 'but in order to put the matter to rest, no. Neither of us sent letters to Professor Macnee, Mr. Plummer.'

'Sorry. I felt like I had to ask. And please call me Gordie.'

'I shall try,' I said.

'May I call you Amelia?'

I levelled a withering gaze at him, which he seemed not to acknowledge, and sighed, 'If you must.' I suppose it is impossible to reverse two centuries of poor North American manners in one afternoon.

'Thank you, Amelia,' he said. 'Now that we're all friends, I hope you won't mind if I ask whether or not you have the professor's letter.'

'I have already told you — '

'No, not the threatening letter, the one

written by Cecil. The letter upon which he based his theory.'

'Robert Cecil?' I asked. 'The Queen's courtier?'

'Oh, you've heard of him,' Mr. Plummer rejoined.

As would have any educated Briton. 'What is this letter?' I asked.

'Well, the professor had wanted to keep the details of it under wraps until his book was completed, but I guess it won't hurt to tell anyone now.' Mr. Plummer leaned in closer, as though afraid of being overheard by someone. 'It says in plain language that Queen Elizabeth and William Shakespeare were one and the same person.'

'A hoax, surely,' I opined.

'It bears the signature of Robert Cecil, who identifies himself as Secretary of State for both Queen Elizabeth and King James. The professor spent almost a year authenticating it. He compared it against samples of Cecil's handwriting from other letters and it matched. He had the parchment examined for age. There is no question that the letter is real.'

'And you have seen this letter?'

'I have, and when the time was right, the professor was going to let everyone see it.' Gordon Plummer — *Gordie* — shook his head. 'I have a terrible feeling that letter is why he was killed.'

'That would certainly explain why his room was ransacked,' I said. 'Inspector Islington should know this.'

'Who?'

'The CID officer who has been assigned to the murder case. He is the one who believes Hathaway Broughton to be the killer. He also believes you to be an accomplice, incidentally.'

'Why me?'

'Because you were there. This letter, Mr. Plummer — '

'Gordie, please.'

'*Gordie* . . . did the professor ever tell you how he obtained it?'

'Professor Macnee collected books from the Elizabethan era, and he discovered it in the binding of one of them.'

'Somebody hid it in an old book?' Harry asked.

'No, it was part of the binding itself.

According to the professor, old parchments were often reused in such fashion back then.'

Or perhaps somebody hoped to preserve it for the future, realizing the letter's potentially explosive significance, I thought. But there was another, perhaps more pertinent question that I felt compelled to ask: 'Mr. Plu . . . Gordie, now that you have our stories, are you really planning to follow us all the way to Stratford?'

'Well, Amelia, if as you say the police in London believe that I am involved in this, it might be a good idea for me to disappear for a while.'

'So here we are,' I muttered.

'Here we are,' Gordon Plummer agreed.

The train's wheels picked the sentiment up and began to sound alarmingly like a rhythmic, metallic, taunting voice repeating over and over: *here we are; here we are; here we are; here we are* . . .

From that point until we approached Stratford, none of us contributed much to the discourse. Instead of worrying about the Canadian, I turned my attention to the train window and watched as more of the verdant countryside of England rolled past. Approaching our destination, the Warwickshire sun seemed brighter and warmer than was achievable within the smoky, teeming confines of London. It bathed the landscape in long golden rays.

After we had pulled into the Stratford-upon-Avon station and detrained under the long pediment-shaped roof, I checked with the station master regarding possible lodgings in the village, or town, or whatever Stratford considered itself, obtaining the address of an establishment called the Tudor Rose. Before long, the three of us were sharing an open coach that was bouncing its way toward the centre of Stratford-upon-Avon.

We soon arrived at the Tudor Rose, a half-timber edifice situated near a spectacular Gothic market fountain and clock, just as the sun was entertaining its first thoughts of retiring for the afternoon. Once inside, it took little time to secure our rooms from the landlord, a rather stern-looking Welshman named Emrys Price. If Mr. Price thought it strange that three people were travelling together with minimal baggage, he said nothing of it, particularly since he received payment for three separate rooms. The first-floor rooms, just up the stairs from the foyer, proved to be small but clean, and were near each other, if not lined up in a row. It appeared to be a most satisfactory arrangement, particularly the promise that a hot breakfast would be included as part of the accommodations. Would that more inns and hostelries included this consideration.

We each repaired to our rooms, having agreed to meet again in an hour and find a suitable restaurant for dinner. Harry and Gordon Plummer disappeared behind their doors, and I took advantage of the time to unlace my shoes and rest on the bed. I turned my head and gazed out of the small rectangular leaded window. Bathed in the orange glow of the waning sun, the city of Stratford was a beautiful sight unlike any to be found back in London.

Once more unto the breach, dear friends, once more, the voice of my old theatrical mentor Laurence Delancey echoed inside my mind. Yet as I heard it, I had the most terrible sense of foreboding.

Into what breach, exactly, was I about to leap?

7

The small eating house that had been recommended for dinner by Mr. Price proved to be perfectly suitable, and the rest of the evening passed without incident, luckily. I retired to my room a bit after ten, leaving Harry and Gordon Plummer to fend for themselves. I was, frankly, exhausted. Unfortunately, it was the manner of exhaustion that causes me to fall asleep quickly, but awaken again only a few hours later and remain somewhere between the states of slumber and awareness throughout the night.

My first awakening came as the moon was high and bright enough to send its beams through the window into the room. I rose and moved to the window to close the curtains, though before I did I caught sight of the dark figure of a man moving below in the eerie blue glow. I could not see him clearly, but he appeared to hold a candle as he crept about. Not knowing what else to do, I rapped on the pane, which caused the figure to look up toward me. After hastily extinguishing his candle, the man vanished into the shadows. *No more yielding but a dream*, I thought, for perhaps that was all it had been.

Yawning, I closed the curtains and returned to bed, where I remained until the morning sun had replaced its night-time counterpart, and was now effectively penetrating the curtains. Despite feeling a measure of exhaustion still, I rolled out of bed, knowing that I could hardly spend the rest of the day there. After freshening and dressing, I made my way down to the breakfast nook. Gordon Plummer was already there, poking a sausage with his fork and sipping a cup of steaming coffee.

'Amelia,' he said, standing as I approached (though forgetting to remove the napkin that he had tucked into his collar), 'I trust you slept well.'

'Well enough,' I said, sitting down and ordering a cup of coffee and a soft-boiled egg from a young woman whose heart seemed not in taking orders for breakfast.

Once she had repaired to the kitchen, I asked: 'Were you up at all last night, Mr. Plummer?'

'No, why?'

'In the middle of the night I swore I saw a man creeping around outside the house.'

'The landlord, most likely,' he said.

Or my imagination, equally likely.

Soon Harry made his way down to join us, a particularly buoyant spring in his tread. 'Good morning, my girl!' he cried as he seated himself at the table. Turning to Mr. Plummer, he brightly added, 'How's it keepin', matey?'

'You are certainly in a fine mood this morning,' I commented.

'Ooohhh, lord love a duck if that weren't the best bed I've laid me bones on in a dog's age! An' then I come down here and what do I see for breakfast but sausages! *Gor*, I may just move in here!'

After ordering and then consuming with gusto a breakfast so sizeable that I began to wonder if he was going to burst the buttons of his new coat, Harry leaned back in his chair with a beatific smile.

'Only one thing could make this day better,' he declared, 'and that's goin' to see sweet Will 'imself. What d'you say, Amelia?'

'Of course I would like to see the village,' I replied, 'but I should first pay a visit to Mary Chelish, since that is the reason I am here. You go on, Harry, and then you will be able to give me a guided tour of the church later.'

'All right, ducks.' Turning to Mr. Plummer, he asked: 'What about you, then?'

'Actually, I would prefer accompanying Mrs. Watson,' he replied.

'What for?' I asked pointedly. 'You don't know Mary Chelish.'

'You can introduce me.'

'The truth is, I don't know her, either.'

'Then we are on equal footing.'

'I'll leave it to you two to figger things out,' Harry said, rising from the table. 'Ta ta, Amelia.' With that he turned and danced his way out of the hotel.

'Mr. Plu — Gordie,' I began, 'this is something of a personal matter. Mrs. Chelish's husband has disappeared, and — '

'A missing persons case,' he interrupted.

'Then I insist on coming with you. I may be able to locate the man. I am a detective, after all.'

I remained sceptical that his presence would accomplish anything but confusion, but I was unable to formulate an argument against it. Even if I had been able to do so, I doubt it would have worked, since despite his vague North American manner, Gordon Plummer seemed highly skilled at obtaining what he wanted. 'Oh, very well,' I said.

The young woman, whose name I learned was Glynis, arrived to take our plates, and I took that opportunity to ask her for directions to the address I had for the Chelish residence. 'I'll ask Uncle Emrys to help you.' She disappeared into the kitchen, and minutes later our landlord emerged, looking as sombre and dour as an executioner. 'My niece tells me you need directions to a particular street,' he said.

'I am looking for Bull Street, Mr. Price.'

After giving very concise directions to the street in question, the landlord added, 'I doubt you'll have any trouble finding it.

A blind person would be hard pressed to get lost in Stratford.'

★   ★   ★

Slightly over an hour later, after Gordon Plummer and I had hiked around and around in circles down narrow streets, back and forth across bridges, and past rows of houses, hedges and shops, I vowed to change my name to Lady Justice, since I clearly was blind. At long last, completely by chance, we came upon a sign reading Bull Street.

'That wasn't so hard, was it?' the Canadian asked.

I chose not to answer.

Number 319 Bull Street, the abode of Mary and Graham Chelish, was a simple brick house with a lower front window framed in bright blue, and a door of matching hue, upon which I rapped. It took three tries, but at last I heard the sounds of a lock being slipped on the other side.

The woman who answered the door was rather short and slight, and for a moment I became convinced that I must have come to the wrong address, for I could not discern much of a resemblance to my friend Beth, who was her sister. 'Yes?' she said, looking back and forth between me and Gordon Plummer.

'Mary Chelish?' I asked.

'Yes, who are you?'

'My name is Amelia Watson. I am a long-time friend of Beth's, and she asked if I might, well, assist you with your problem.'

Her eyes lit up. 'Yes, of course, please come in!' she said, opening the door fully and stepping back to allow us to enter. 'I am sorry, but I was not expecting you to actually turn up on the doorstep.'

'Yes, and I do apologize for not giving you any notice,' I said. 'Circumstances were such that, well, here I am. I do hope I am not intruding.'

'No, not at all.' The house into which we stepped was rather small but comfortable, if a bit dark. There seemed to be a candlestick or candelabra on virtually every surface. Closing the door behind us, Mary turned to Mr. Plummer and said, 'And you, sir, must be Dr. Watson.'

I had opened my mouth to correct her assumption, but before I could speak, to my horror I heard the Canadian say, 'Yes, that's right.' My mouth continued opening until it must have resembled a train tunnel.

'You're somewhat younger than I was expecting,' Mary said of my 'husband'.

'People remark upon that all the time,' he replied in a reasonable facsimile of a London accent. 'The fact that I don't look my age. It's the effects of clean living, I suppose.'

Now I covered my gaping mouth with both hands.

'Sit down, please,' Mary bade us, and we took our seats on a rather cramped sofa. 'May I offer you some tea?'

'That would be lovely, Mrs. Chelish, thank you,' I said.

'Please, call me Mary, and I shall call you Amelia. And you, sir, what shall I call you?'

'James.'

'*John!*' I cried.

'Oh, yes, sorry. James is a nickname. Please call me John.'

'All right, John,' Mary said, and then she retreated into the back of the house. Once I was convinced she was out of earshot, I turned on Gordon Plummer. 'What do you think you are *doing*?' I whispered furiously. 'Why did you tell her you were my husband?'

'Don't you think she might consider it strange that you are travelling with a man other than your husband?' he whispered back. 'Besides, if they believe me to be a famous detective, they will be more forthcoming with information.'

'Sherlock Holmes is a detective; my husband is *not*.'

'He is almost a detective.'

'And you are coming perilously close to being a — ' I snapped my mouth shut again as I heard Mary's footsteps nearing the room, and forced myself to smile as she came in carrying a tray with an ornate teapot and three cups. 'I already had the water on the boil,' she said, setting the tray down on a small table and pouring. The tea was strong and good; and while Mary and I added milk and sugar, as any respectable English native would do,

Gordon Plummer took his black. 'I'm sorry I do not have any biscuits at present,' Mary said.

'Please do not concern yourself over it,' I responded. 'We had an ample breakfast at the hotel.'

'Well, then,' Gordon Plummer blundered ahead, 'suppose we talk about this problem, eh wot?'

'I'm sorry?' Mary said.

'Mary, could I trouble you for some lemon?' I asked hastily.

'For the tea? I believe I have some in the kitchen, though I do not usually serve it with milk and sugar.'

'It is not for me, it is for John.'

'All right, I'll only be a moment,' Mary Chelish said, rising once more and walking out of the room.

'I don't like lemon in my tea,' Gordon Plummer argued after she had gone.

'I don't care! I only wish I had access to cod oil to put in your cup! It is bad enough you pretend to be my husband, but now you blunder your way into her problems! We may be on Bull Street, Mr. Plummer, but this is not a china shop!' If my hushed tirade distressed him in any way, his face did not reveal it, which made me wonder what exactly *was* going on in that chilled Canadian brain.

Mary was back now with a small bowl containing lemon slices, one of which I picked up and twisted forcefully into Mr. Plummer's tea, and secretly hoping it would give him an upset stomach. 'Thank you, dear,' I said to Mary.

'Yes, thank you,' Mr. Plummer muttered, taking a sip and trying to cover a grimace. 'Now then, back to the subject, Mrs. Chelish. Forgive me if I seem a bit forward, but we have been told that your husband has gone missing.' I held my tongue and my breath, and counted silently to ten.

'Yes, it is true. Gray began acting a bit strangely about a year ago, but recently — '

'I'm sorry . . . Gray?' Mr. Plummer interrupted.

'Oh really, *John*, I'm surprised at you,' I said with artificial sweetness. 'Gray is the affectionate diminutive for Graham, just as James is short for John. Surely you should have been able to deduce that.'

Elated at the slight flush that was rising in Mr. Plummer's face, I turned back to Mary and said, 'Do please continue. What has happened recently?'

'Well, Gray has become so distant,' she replied. 'Some days he treats me like a stranger.'

'When did this start?'

'After he began working on a book.'

'He is an author?' I asked.

'By trade he is a candlemaker. From whence the idea for writing a book came, I have no idea. He closes himself up in the attic for hours on end and then goes out for days at a time, ostensibly doing research; but what kind of research, I cannot begin to tell you. All I know is that he claims that this book, when it is published, is going to make him internationally famous and provide us with wealth.'

'Do you know what the book is about?' Mr. Plummer asked.

'That is the strangest thing of all,' Mary replied. 'I do not know many of the details, but it has something to do with the authorship of Shakespeare, of all things.'

Gordon Plummer and I exchanged looks.

'Is Graham a Shakespearean scholar?' I asked.

'Not at all. He was born here and has lived in Stratford all his life, but until recently he never gave any indication that he cared a whit about Shakespeare. If anything, he considered him more of a nuisance for the town because it brought in so many visitors. But without any warning, he became obsessed with the notion that William Shakespeare did not really write the plays.'

I could not help but wonder if some sort of mass hysteria had suddenly engulfed Britain, leaving me as the only denizen of the realm who still believed that the plays and sonnets were actually written by Stratford's greatest son. But even mass hysteria had to have time to gestate. 'You make it sound like he simply went to bed one night and awakened the next day a man obsessed,' I said.

Mary Chelish sighed. 'No, in retrospect I can see that there were warning signs, which I failed to recognize at the time. Gray began forgetting things, unimportant things at first. But then he began to forget more important matters, such as our wedding anniversary. Then he seemed to shift from simple absent-mindedness to pure apathy, as though he was too preoccupied to care about anything. One day he decided he was too busy to go into work, and that was that. He never went in again. The shop quickly closed.'

'Oh dear. How are you subsisting?'

'We had some money saved — enough for a while, but it is dwindling. Whenever I would bring up the subject of finances, Gray would tell me not to worry, that his book would provide the answer to our problems.'

'So he began spending his days here in the house, working on his book at the expense of consideration to you?' I asked, knowing the feeling.

'He would sometimes go out and visit the lending library, or simply walk around the village, but he would always come back. Then he began to disappear for periods of time, sometimes for an afternoon, sometimes an entire day. He would always return, though sometimes it would be late into the night; but he would never offer an explanation as to where he had been. I confess that there were times when I assumed the worst.'

'You mean another woman?' Mr. Plummer asked.

Mary nodded and her tightly closed lips quivered, as though she were struggling to prevent a sob. 'It turned out to be rather more innocent, thank heavens,' she said. 'He was stealing away to meet with a man from the Memorial Theatre, a Shakespearean scholar who acts as a historical consultant for the productions that are done there. I do not know this for certain, but I think that the man . . . Graves, or Greaves, I believe his name is . . . may have banished Gray from the place.'

I took the last comment to imply that Mr. Graves-or-Greaves had not agreed with Graham Chelish's conclusions. It would probably be worth a visit to the Memorial Theatre to speak with the man.

'Whenever he spoke of the man thereafter, it was to rage on about his idiocy. He also began ranting about flowers.'

'Flowers?'

'At first I thought he was considering

opening a floral shop to replace the candle business, but it sounded more like he was claiming that a flower was the source of all his problems. That was when I began to fear for his mental condition, but there was nothing I could do about it. I asked him to see a doctor, and he would only laugh. Then on Saturday last, nearly a fortnight ago now, Gray said he was going out and told me not to wait up. That is the last I have seen of him.'

'Mary,' Mr. Plummer began, familiarly, 'I do not wish to alarm you by asking this, but is it possible your husband could have met with harm?'

'Why do you think I have been so distraught?' she declared, and rightly so, for it was a rather foolish question. 'Anything is possible.'

'You have, of course, notified the police?' I asked.

'Immediately, but I have heard nothing from them. I believe the police think he simply went off to do 'man things' for which he did not require my permission or approval.'

'Have the police chatted with all of

your husband's friends to see if they know of his whereabouts?' my 'husband' asked.

'Gray does not have many friends,' Mary answered.

'Then have they checked with the station master to see if he bought a ticket out of the city, or with any public transportation drivers who might have recalled having him as a fare?'

'I believe they have.'

'I see.' Gordon Plummer's expression indicated he had not anticipated that his outlined plan of action would already have been attempted.

'You know, Mary,' I said, trying to sound comforting, 'John's friend Sherlock Holmes has a saying that he is forever quoting regarding the solutions to conundrums: 'Once you have eliminated the impossible, whatever is left, no matter how improbable, must be the solution.' Can you think of anyplace, no matter how improbable, but short of impossible, that Graham might have gone?'

'He might have gone *anywhere*, Amelia. That is the problem.'

Before I could respond in any way,

comforting or otherwise, there came the sound of a knocking at the door. 'Perhaps that is the police,' Mary said, rising to answer it. Mr. Plummer and I remained where we were.

'I may never forgive you for this,' I hissed to him once Mary was out of earshot.

'For what?'

'Carrying on this impersonation of my husband in order to delude a vulnerable woman!'

The self-proclaimed John H. Watson opened his mouth to reply, but what appeared to come out was a woman's cry. It was not the voice of Mr. Plummer, but rather of Mary, from the next room. We both rose and dashed into the foyer.

Standing in the doorway of the Chelish home was a policeman; and with him, appearing to be in some kind of stupor, was another man of some forty-five years of age, with gently greying hair and a haunted expression. His dark eyes looked around the house as though he was unfamiliar with it, and only seemed to focus when he turned his gaze to Gordon Plummer. I, however, could not spend a lot of time puzzling out the man's expression; beside me, Mary Chelish appeared to deflate and slumped to the floor. 'Mary!' I cried, rushing to her. 'What is the matter?'

'I cannot withstand much more of this,' she said. 'First he disappears, then he simply turns up like a ha'penny on the street.'

At once I understood the situation. The befuddled-looking man in front of me had to be Graham Chelish.

8

As I glanced down at the prostrate figure of Mary Chelish, my relief that her husband had safely turned up was completely overwhelmed by the rush of anger I felt toward him, rationally or otherwise. 'Mr. Chelish, do you have any idea what you have put your wife through?' I demanded. The man gazed back at me as though I were a unicorn.

'Please, Amelia, it is fine,' Mary gasped, rising to a sitting position.

'Not by half, it isn't,' I said. 'Mr. Chelish, you do not know me, but I am a friend of your wife's and I believe you owe her an apology for your reckless actions.' Graham Chelish appeared monumentally unimpressed by either my words or my scolding manner. Instead he was staring at Gordon Plummer with a focus that had been absent in his perusal of me only seconds earlier.

'What are you doing in my house?' Chelish asked.

'I am here with my wife,' Mr. Plummer lied. 'I am Dr. Watson.'

'*The* Dr. Watson?' the policeman asked, his face suddenly brightening.

'I am certain there are others, but I am the author of the stories of Sherlock Holmes, yes.'

I had to turn away and once more clamp a hand over my mouth, lest I ruin the game by blurting out the truth (which had long ago fled this room like a mouse scurrying into a crack in the wall in search of safety).

'I see,' Chelish said, in such a tone as implied that he saw no better than a blind man.

'Constable, can you tell us what happened?' Mr. Plummer asked.

'Well, sir, we found this gentleman inside Trinity Church, where he shouldn't've been, I'm afraid.'

'You mean in a private area?' Mary asked.

'I mean on the grave, ma'am.'

Within the confines of Trinity Church of Stratford, *the grave* could only mean one thing. 'He was standing on Shakespeare's grave?'

'If we hadn't come along when we did, he might've been standing *in* it,' the constable replied. 'He had a jemmy in his hand and was holding it like he was thinking of smashing through the stone and opening her up.'

'Gray!' Mary cried, using the sofa to pull herself upright.

'We stopped him before any real harm was done,' the constable went on, 'and since he appeared to be suffering from an affliction that clouded his senses, the sergeant felt there would be little reason to haul him into the gaol.'

As though he had suddenly become charged by electricity, Graham Chelish violently shook off the policeman's grip and shouted: 'Unhand me, you oaf! Are citizens to be arrested now for conducting research?'

'Gray, please . . . ' Mary begged.

Chelish began frantically looking about the room as though he were trapped in a cell. 'Not one of you knows what I know, *not one of you!*' he cried. 'I have learned things, things that nobody knows. I found where they are hidden. They tried to squirrel them away in the dusty corners of the Bodleian, but they couldn't hide them from me!'

'The Bodleian Library?' I said. 'In Oxford?'

'Gray, is that where you have been?' Mary asked.

Chelish acted as though she had never spoken and continued to rant. 'The clues led me back here . . . here . . . where the ultimate truth lies buried in that church.' He then froze as though suddenly stricken, and as I watched, the curtain of torpor once more rang down around him. He regarded me with an uncomprehending expression, and then turned his gaze to his wife, to whom he meekly asked: 'Are you ill, Mary? You're pallid.'

'Don't worry about me, Gray,' she said weakly. 'Please come and sit down. Lay down if you like.'

'Yes, I am a bit weary.' He shuffled off to the day room, with Mary following, holding her head in her hands as she walked.

'That one needs to see a doctor,' the constable said. Then turning to Mr.

Plummer, he added, 'Good thing you're here, sir.'

The Canadian looked confused. 'It is?'

'He means because you *are* a doctor, *John*,' I rejoined. 'You can examine him here.'

'Oh. Oh yes, at once,' Mr. Plummer said, scampering into the next room.

'Sad to see a gent's mind sail out of the harbour like that,' the constable said.

'Speaking for Mrs. Chelish,' I said, 'I'd like to thank you for not mistaking his instability with premeditated criminality.'

'Well, ma'am, like I said, there seemed little reason to haul him into the gaol, especially since we believe that the other one, the fellow who was with him, was the mastermind behind it.'

A terrible apprehension overcame me. 'Other one?'

'Little gent, about this tall,' the policeman said, holding out his hand precisely to Harry Benbow's height. 'He had a bag of tools, which he dropped when he ran. We figure he was the one trying to break into the grave, and he was using this poor addled blighter to help him.'

'And this little fellow got away?' I asked numbly.

'Dashed away like a little rabbit. But we'll find him. There are not a lot of places to hide in Stratford.'

'What a comfort.'

'I have to be going now, ma'am. If the gent in there proves to be any more trouble, you can always call on us.'

'Thank you, Constable . . . I am afraid I did not get your name.'

The policeman sighed, like it was an unpleasant question. 'It's Constable, ma'am.'

'I understand that, but I am endeavouring to learn your given name.'

The man sighed again. 'Constable is my name, ma'am. Derrick Constable.'

'So you are Constable Constable?'

'You see, ma'am, when I was a lad, everybody called me Constable instead of Derrick, so I guess it got planted into my head that this would be a fine line of work. I didn't think it all the way through, though. But there's naught to be done about it now. Now if you'll excuse me, ma'am.' Constable Constable gave me a tidy salute, turned, and took his leave.

The front door had hardly closed behind him when Mary Chelish came back into the room, cradling her head in her hands. 'I am at my wits' end, Amelia,' she said, seating herself on the small sofa. 'I simply do not know what to do about Gray. I can't bring myself to consider institutionalizing him, but neither can I watch over him every hour of the day. How can I even sleep at night knowing that at any moment he might run off again on some personal crusade or other without my knowledge?'

At that moment I wished I could do something to comfort her, but based upon what Constable Constable had just told me, I now had Harry's welfare to worry about. Yet again.

'Is Graham resting?' I asked.

'Yes, and Dr. Watson is looking in on him. What a blessing he accompanied you, Amelia.'

'Yes, isn't it?'

'I am hoping he can obtain something from the chemist's to keep Gray calm.'

And were it really my husband in there and not Gordon Plummer, he would be able to do precisely that. Perhaps I could figure out some way to obtain a draught for Chelish on my own, right after I figured out how to accomplish everything else I had taken upon myself in this ill-advised mission.

As though knowing he was being spoken about, and wishing to hear it for himself, Mr. Plummer emerged from the bedroom and came to us. 'He is resting,' he announced. 'I should not disturb him for a while. Whatever transpired during his escapade, it appears to have worn him out.'

'Can you fetch something for him to keep him quiet and at rest through the night?' Mary begged.

'What sort of something?' Mr. Plummer asked.

'*Darling*,' I said pointedly, 'Mary wishes you to obtain a sleeping draught from the chemist. Perhaps we should go and do that.'

'Um, yes, of course,' Mr. Plummer said.

'We shall check back in with you later,' I told Mary; and, practically pulling my 'husband' through the door behind me, I took leave of the house. Once outside, I muttered: 'Could things possibly go any further awry?'

'I think things are progressing very well indeed,' Gordon Plummer replied. 'I don't know why you are so concerned.'

'Half of Stratford thinks we are married! They think you are Dr. John Watson! What's more, it would appear that Harry is wanted by the police. The only way on earth we could be progressing is if we were on the road to Bedlam!'

'You don't know that it was Mr. Benbow in the church,' he said.

'You don't know Mr. Benbow,' I replied. I had no doubt whatsoever that Harry had not been there for malicious or felonious reasons; but given his brilliance for being in the wrong place at the wrong time, I also had no doubt it had been he who was seen by Constable Constable.

'Look on the bright side,' Mr. Plummer went on. 'We have found the missing man, haven't we? That was, I believe, the objective for coming here.'

'One of them. Our next objective must

be to proceed to the nearest chemist to obtain a calming draught for Graham Chelish. That will be up to you, Mr. Plummer.'

'You are leaving me to my own devices?'

'Yes. I must go to the police in order to find out exactly what sort of trouble Harry has gotten himself into this time. Since I cannot stop you from brandishing my husband's name, perhaps in this instance it will be for a good cause. You are Dr. John H. Watson, visiting from London, and you have stumbled on an emergency for which you need a draught. Whatever the chemist opts to give you, take it, but say you've not used that particular powder before and must refresh your knowledge of the dosage. The chemist will tell you. Once you have it, take it immediately to the Chelish house. After that, you are on your own.'

'I'm glad you have such faith in me, Amelia,' he said.

'Mr. Plummer — '

'Gordie, please.'

'No, I am sorry, I will not call you

Gordie, particularly now that you have made it uncomfortably expedient to continue calling you *John*. As for faith in you, I have as much as a shipwreck victim has in the buoyancy of a plank of wood that floats by. In other words, what choice do I have?'

He looked chastened at that.

'I am sorry if I offended you . . . *Gordon* . . . but this is not a Boy's Own adventure.'

'I understand,' he said quietly. 'Is there anything else?'

'Yes. We in England do not say *oaut*.'

'What is *oaut*?'

'For Canadians, it is the opposite of 'in'. If you must continue impersonating my husband, please practise pronouncing the word correctly. It is *owt*.'

I was gratified to watch him spend the next few seconds practising the word, coming closer each time. It would have to do.

After co-ordinating with Mr. Plummer when and where we would meet up later in the day, I sent him off on his assignment while I set out for police headquarters which, according to the shopkeeper from whom I asked directions, was located in Sheep Street.

The remarkable thing about Shakespeare's natal village is that nothing is very far away from anything else, particularly if one is accustomed to the sprawling, rambling, sometimes dark and deadly maze that comprises London. The police station proved to be an easy building to spot, and as I entered was gratified to find Constable Constable standing there. 'Fancy seeing you again so soon, ma'am,' he said, bobbing his head by way of a formal greeting.

'Oh, I am so glad that you are here, Constable,' I said, happy that the pretence which had arisen in my mind during the walk here would be delivered to a familiar face. 'That man you said you saw in the church with Graham, you said he was a diminutive fellow?'

'Yes, ma'am. What about him?'

'I may have seen him.'

He came to attention and alertness as though suddenly infused with an electrical charge. 'Indeed?'

'As I left the Chelish house I saw a man loitering about on the street, and it appeared as though he was surveilling the house.'

'Can you describe him further?'

'As you said, he was a small man and had thick dark hair, and I believe he was wearing a grey suit.'

'Blimey, that's him!'

'I shouted at him,' I went on, cheerfully deceiving the officer (though I preferred to think of it as *acting*), 'and once he realized he had been detected, he turned and ran in a strange rolling gait, almost like a dance.'

'Madam, I wish all our witnesses were as sharp and observant as you,' Constable Constable said.

'I want to help if I can,' I said, smiling at him like the ingénue of a penny dreadful melodrama. What I was really doing, of course, was ascertaining for certain that it had been Harry the policeman saw in the church. Based upon his eager confirmation of my description, there was now no doubt in my mind.

'Did you see where he ran to?'

'Down the street, though I am a visitor to Stratford and I cannot be certain which street.'

'We'll put all our efforts into finding the little blighter. Pardon my language, ma'am.'

'Of course. But Constable, what will you do with the man when you find him? He appeared to be such a harmless little fellow that I would hate to think of him being brutalized.'

'We are not London, madam,' Constable Constable said soberly. 'We don't brutalize suspects here. All I want to do is talk to him and see what his story is about being in the church and looking like he was going to break into the tomb of our beloved poet. I'll inform the sergeant right away and we'll take it from here.'

I left the police station with the understanding that I had to find Harry before any of the police did, but where to begin looking in a foreign town? He had said at breakfast was that he wished to visit the church of Shakespeare's burial, which he clearly had. That seemed as good a place as any to start the search.

Following the directions given to me by an idle cabman (whose offer to take me there I politely refused, having spent too much time in vehicles over the last few days), I soon arrived at Holy Trinity Church, which was located on the banks of the gently flowing Avon. In appearance it was like nearly every other stone church of the late Norman period. It was certainly not as striking an edifice as the Shakespeare Memorial Theatre, which was located only a short distance upriver. The theatre was a remarkably eccentric Gothic pile complete with a massive rotunda, sweeping arches and a medieval tower, all warring in such a cacophony of visual dissonance that one might assume its construction had been commissioned by a mad Bavarian king.

The approach to Holy Trinity itself was down a long walkway through a church-yard whose ancient headstones looked as lonely and foreboding as any ever encountered by a Dickens character. The sombre stillness of the place was, however, shattered by the movements of two uniformed policemen, one of whom was stationed at the ornate wooden door of the church. 'Is there a problem?' I asked him.

'No ma'am, just routine patrol,' he replied, though I doubted it. He and the other were looking for Harry. 'Go in if you like.'

'Thank you.' I entered the structure feeling not so much reverence for the man I knew to be interred there, but a cold, gnawing fear for Harry's safety. There was yet another policeman inside, though he merely nodded as I made my way up the nave toward the chancel, which was cordoned off. The Shakespeare Memorial was on the wall of the left side.

I do not know exactly what I had been expecting; perhaps an array of stage lights and a curtain proclaiming its importance to the world. But as I stared at the rather unprepossessing bust of a full-faced, balding, middle-aged man staring placidly out from a granite frame, I could not help but feel that a poet of such monumental proportions was getting short shrift from his memorial. Then again, this was erected shortly after Shakespeare's death, at which time he was known to the playgoing public of London, and to the denizens of Stratford, but not yet to the world at large. So many monuments outweigh the men they commemorate; here, the converse seemed true.

The actual grave of William Shakespeare was on the floor of the chancel and covered with a large grey slab inscribed with a decidedly un-Shakespearian bit of doggerel:

Good frend for Jesus sake forebeare,
To digg the dust enclosed heare.
Blese be the man that spares thes stones,
And curst be he that moves my bones.

Charity mandated the assumption that, had Shakespeare himself written this epitaph, it was only the first draft. Regardless, the curse had achieved its objective: Shakespeare's bones had not been moved to make room for newer tenants. Examining the grave, I realized that while coming here was valuable in terms of venerating England's greatest playwright, it had been a waste of precious time in terms of finding Harry. What had I been expecting, a treasure map left for me in his hand?

With a sigh I turned away from the modest shrine to William Shakespeare and walked back up the nave, stopping to take a seat in a pew. The church was quiet and empty, and almost indescribably peaceful. I gazed upon the ornately crafted stained-glass windows and closed my eyes. I do not know how long I was thus seated, but upon hearing the hushed voice in my left ear, I started.

'A place of serenity, is it not?' it said.

Without turning back to look, I whispered, 'Harry, is that you?'

'I am afraid not.'

Slowly I turned around to see the smiling face of Inspector Horatio Islington in the pew directly behind me.

9

After I had recovered from the shock of seeing the man where he ought not to be, and having appeared out of nowhere like a magician's rabbit to boot, I managed to say: 'Inspector, what on earth are you doing here?'

'Working, dear lady, working,' he replied amiably. 'I am continuing my investigation.'

'In Stratford?'

'Indeed. My jurisdiction extends beyond the confines of London when the occasion demands it.'

'In other words, you have followed me.'

He smiled. 'Shall we take our leave of this place, inspiring though it is, and find another location in which to continue our conversation?'

Before a quarter hour had passed, we were both seated at a table in the corner of a comfortable tea shop. 'Would you mind if I asked a frank question, Inspector?' I said.

'By all means, Mrs. Watson. If the answer is mine to give, it shall be yours.'

'You are not a member of the CID, are you?'

'I assure you, dear lady, I am.'

'Very well, you are. But that is not all you are, is it?'

'What else would I be?'

'My guess is that you work directly for the Home Office, for which your position as a police inspector is merely a cover.'

Inspector Islington smiled. 'A deduction as astute as it is provocative, dear lady,' he replied. 'And as it so happens, I have been authorized by my superior to answer your question, since my superior happens to be a mutual friend of ours.'

'A mutual friend,' I uttered, and a second later I realized what he was saying. 'Good heavens, you work for Mycroft Holmes.'

Inspector Islington smiled again and bowed his head to me. 'I have the honour of serving the Empire through a special department of the Home Office headed by Mr. Holmes,' he confessed. 'As of yet no one has come up with a satisfactory name for this department, so until such occurrence happens we are simply known as M Division — M standing for Mycroft. Anything that falls outside the normal purview of police or military activity eventually comes to us. We report directly to Mr. Holmes, who in turn is the liaison with the Crown.'

'All of this sounds like a very secretive business,' I said, raising my teacup to my lips and blowing the steam away.

'Oh, it is, it is. Even my colleagues at the Yard do not know the full details of my activities for M Division.'

'Then why are you revealing it to me?'

The inspector smiled warmly. 'As I have said, Mr. Holmes has authorized me to do so because he says you are to be trusted, which is not a word commonly heard in his lexicon. He also believes your participation might be crucial in bringing this case to a successful conclusion.'

I confess that I was of two minds upon hearing that: while I was not completely comfortable with the way this situation was evolving, it would be disingenuous of me not to admit that I felt a little bit thrilled — heaven help me — upon hearing in what esteem my past service to His Majesty was being held.

'Since you are already involved in the matter of the murder of Professor Todhunter Macnee,' he went on, 'it would seem like the most logical thing in the world for us to join heads, as it were.'

'I do not know what I can tell you about it that you do not already know.'

'You can tell me what drew you here to Stratford-on-Avon. Unless contradicted, I must assume it was not to see the sights.'

'In large part it was to visit the sister of an old friend who was dealing with a problem that is completely unrelated to the tragedy of Professor Macnee.'

'I see. And the smaller part?'

'Frankly, Inspector, it was to get away from you.'

He seemed genuinely surprised at that. 'Why would you feel threatened by me? It was you who volunteered to come in to see me in the first place, was it not?'

'Yes, but that was only to ... ' I stopped immediately, realizing that I would have to tell him about my concern for Harry, who in the guise of Hathaway

Broughton was still at the top of his suspect list.

Inspector Islington examined me carefully for a moment, his placid face dissolving into a rather discomforting mask of focus and intelligence. 'Back in the church, before turning to face me, you asked if I was 'Harry',' he said. 'You would not by chance have been referring to 'Har Har Harry', the author of that grievously misspelled letter in your home, would you? A man we both alternately know as Hathaway Broughton, esquire?'

'I did not like you reading my mail, Inspector.'

'Then, dear lady, you shouldn't have left it lying about!' he rejoined cheerfully. 'Come, come, Mrs. Watson, it really would be best to tell me everything.'

I sighed, knowing he was right. It was time to stop hiding, stop prevaricating, and let someone of authority know what was going on. 'Would you be so good as to hand me that tray of scones?' I asked, and he did. Taking one, I started at the beginning and told the inspector everything about the matter that had managed to envelop me, including the fact that Harry had already managed to get himself implicated in a transgression here in Stratford, though I did not mention the fact that the man in whose company he had been spotted was Graham Chelish. I felt that Mary had troubles enough with which to contend without adding the presence of Inspector Islington in her life, particularly since her problems were unrelated to the murder of Professor Macnee. Neither did I mention that Gordon Plummer had assumed my husband's identity. Explaining my complicity in that particular ruse would have been too embarrassing, particularly if somehow it got back to John.

Inspector Islington listened carefully, interrupting me only to ask: 'What do you know about this Canadian chap?'

'Only what he has told me. He is a private detective, and his involvement was that he had been hired by Professor Macnee to investigate certain threats that had been made against him.'

'But you do now know for a fact that he is who and what he says he is?'

'I know he cannot pronounce the word 'out', which does point to his being a Canadian. Good heavens, Inspector, are you implying that *he* is a suspect?'

'At present I cannot say, though anyone who was in the presence of the late Professor Macnee should at the very least be questioned. Do you know where Mr. Plummer is now?'

'No, not precisely. Somewhere in the city, I believe.'

'And your friend, Mr. Benbow? Do you know where he is?'

'Believe me, Inspector, I wish I did know.'

'You seem rather devoted to him.'

'I met him when I was very young, and working in a theatrical company. He became a mentor to me, both creatively and in protecting me from a few of the other actors. I was then a mere slip of a girl, you understand. These days, though, our roles have reversed, and I occasionally feel like his nanny, preventing him from chasing a ball into a busy street. It is hard to describe, except to say that despite all the complications, the world becomes more entertaining in his company.'

The inspector finished his last sip of tea and stood up to leave. 'When you come across your two compatriots, you will notify me at once, I trust,' he said.

'I was rather hoping simply to collect them and leave Stratford,' I replied. 'After all, the personal matter of which I spoke appears to have been resolved.'

'That could lead to an unfortunate situation with the local constabulary regarding Mr. Benbow, a situation which I am confident I could resolve to the satisfaction of all.'

'Very well. But how do I notify you?'

'You can get a message to me through the police headquarters here in the village. They have a telephone — as, I believe, does the Tudor Rose. That would be the most exigent way.' Pulling a small purse out of his pocket, he opened it and withdrew two shillings and placed them on the table. 'Good day, Mrs. Watson,' he said, and was gone from the tea shop before I had a chance to say anything further. It was only later, once I had left the shop and gotten outside into the fresh air of Stratford, that my head cleared enough to realize that at no time had I informed Inspector Islington where in the town we were staying. How did he know I was at the Tudor Rose? I was beginning to feel that I was swimming in waters far too deep for me.

Having no better idea of where to look for Harry, I set out for the hotel, a journey that took little time since I was getting my directional bearings for the town. Emrys Price was nowhere to be found this time of day, though Glynis was running a ewbank over the carpet in the day room. 'Excuse me, dear,' I said, 'but have you by any chance seen my travelling companion?'

'Which one?' the girl asked.

'The rather small fellow.'

'No, I haven't seen him since this morning. But there was another man hanging about outside earlier.'

'Oh? Was he tall and on the portly side and white-haired?'

'He was white-haired, but not portly. Quite short, too. Walked with a limp.'

Based on the description, I had a

strong suspicion as to who this mysterious figure might have been. 'What happened to him?' I asked.

'I've no idea. I came out onto the porch to get a better look at him, but he was nowhere to be found. I walked the entire front of the house and into the side yard and garden, but he had vanished.'

'Thank you, dear,' I said, then went up the stairs (which unlike the floors below had plainly not been swept for quite some time) and walked to the door of Harry's room, waiting a moment until I heard the sound of the sweeper being dragged back and forth across the carpet, before rapping soundly on the door. 'Harry,' I stage-whispered, 'open the door. I know you are in there.'

The door cracked open and Harry peered out. 'C'mon in, ducks,' he whispered, opening the door just widely enough for me to pass through before closing it and locking it again. His hair was wet and a towel was draped around his shoulders, but I could still see traces of something white streaking his temples. 'It's plaster dust,' he said, walking to the water bowl on the table beside his bed, dipping in one corner of the towel, and briskly rubbing the sides of his head. 'I had to high-tail it away from that church like Jack Robinson, and since the local peelers had seen me, I needed a disguise. I ran past a building site and took a little o' the plaster, an' afore you can say Bob's yer uncle, ol' Harry's a greybeard. I think that girl downstairs might o' seen me standin' around, but she din't see me slip in.'

'Well, you can rest a bit easier, Harry. Inspector Islington followed us down here from London, and — '

'*Gor*, he come to pinch me, ha'nt he?'

'No, he believes you are innocent in the Macnee matter, though he does wish to speak with you and Mr. Plummer. He thinks he can even rectify your present trouble with the police. And since we're on the subject, Harry, what on earth *were* you doing trying to break into the grave of Shakespeare?'

'Now, hold on, ducks. How'd you know what happened back there at the blinkin' church? All I said was the peelers were after me.'

'That man you were assisting, or whatever you happened to be doing with him, was Graham Chelish, the missing husband of my friend's sister.'

'No kiddin'? He's the reason you came here in the first place?'

I nodded.

'Small world, ain't it?'

I pulled the room's chair from the corner and repositioned it before sitting down. 'All right, Harry, the stage is yours,' I said. 'Tell me what you were up to.'

He took the towel from around his neck and threw it on his bed, then sat down next to it. 'All I wanted to do was pay my respects to ol' sweet Will,' he began. 'I mean, this is Himself we're talkin' about! Crikey, ducks, I got the shakes just walkin' into the place. I sat meself down in a pew and was lookin' at that bust o' his, when suddenly this bloke shows up carrying a bloomin' pickaxe! He looks like he's gonna start choppin' into the tomb itself! So I comes runnin' up and tries to stop him. I take the pick out of his hand, and then he starts telling me about some great secret buried inside the grave, and he's the only one who's figgered it out, and he's got to prove himself right. Well, now, I'm not about to let some right royal charlie go smashin' into the final resting place of the Swan o' blinkin' Avon! So I tries to talk him out of it. He keeps rabbitin' on about somethin' but he's not makin' not a mole's worth of bloomin' sense.'

'Can you remember anything that he said?'

'Oh, aye. And loony, it was. He said as how it weren't Shakespeare buried in the grave, an' how he's the only one what knows that.'

'Who does he think is there?'

'I din't get the chance to find out, 'cause right then, the coppers rushed in. Well, the bloke shouts out at 'em, kind o' dramatic-like, and then takes off, leavin' me standin' there, holdin' his blinkin' pickaxe! I decided it was best to make my bloomin' exit as well. I chucked the pick in the churchyard and made meself scarce.'

'Do you remember what he shouted,

kind of dramatic-like?' I asked.

'That I got, ducks. He reared back and hollered: 'Away! The foul fiend follows me!' Then he dashed away.'

'The foul fiend?'

'Right. At the time I figgered that's what he was callin' the coppers, but since I've had the time to give it a tiddly, I started wonderin' if he was referrin' to me, accusin' me of being the foul fiend, pretendin' like this whole caper was my idea!'

'If that was the case, Harry, it worked,' I said. 'The foul fiend follows me . . . ' Do you recognize that as a quotation?'

'Sounds a tad familiar, don't it? Maybe the Scottish play.'

'The Scottish play' was the way theatrical people referred to *Macbeth*, believing against all rationality that the very mention of Shakespeare's masterful tragedy carried with it a curse.

'So, ducks, now you know,' Harry said. 'What do we do now?'

'I told Inspector Islington I would notify him when I found you and our Canadian friend. Mr. Plummer should be returning here later, but since the two of us are together, I believe our best course of action would be to go straight to police headquarters.'

'Blimey, the peelers? What for?'

'So you can be cleared of any wrong-doing. Inspector Islington seemed certain that he could convince the locals of your innocence, and the only way he can be reached is through the police station. We must go there and ask for him, even if we have to wait some time for him to arrive.'

'I dunno, ducks. Coppers make me nervous.'

'It's the only way, Harry. You don't want to keep having to sneak around the town in disguise, do you? This way you can walk about without any worries.'

'All right, if you say so, Amelia. Let me get my jacket.'

As we walked downstairs, Harry said, 'Once I'm free and clear to stroll about, though, there's one place I want to pay a call on 'fore we leave.'

'The Shakespeare house?' I asked.

'No, the Filthy Fowl.'

'The *what*?'

'That's what the locals call it. It's really

the Black Bittern, a pub down by the theatre, used by all the play folk. *Gor*, ducks, seein' as how the two of us is play folk, too, why don't we both go?'

Out of the list of things I felt that I had to do, patronizing an establishment called the Filthy Fowl scored at the bottom. 'I really should check in again to see how Mary Chelish is doing,' I said. 'Though I suppose we could try to squeeze in a visit to this Filthy Fowl of yours later this afternoon.'

'That's me girl!' Harry crowed. 'That's what I like about you, luv. When you're around, everything just works out.'

We had no sooner stepped through the door of the Tudor Rose and out onto the porch when I immediately stopped.

'What is it, Amelia?' Harry asked.

'I've just realized that we don't have to go the police station, is all,' I told him.

'Why's that?'

'Because the man we need to see has come to us. He is right over there.'

Standing on the sidewalk leading up to the hotel was Inspector Islington, who smiled and waved at Harry and me.

10

'You know, Inspector,' I sighed as we approached him, 'I am growing weary of being followed by you.'

'A thousand apologies, dear lady.' he replied. 'But I am correct in assuming this is Mr. Harry Benbow, am I not?'

'You are,' Harry said, 'though I got nothin' to do with no murder.'

'I believe you, sir.'

'*Gor*, thank you, guv!' he said, grabbing the inspector's hand and shaking it like a water pump. 'What can ol' Harry do to repay you?'

The inspector's smile became fixed and he leaned slightly toward Harry. 'You can vouchsafe to me, sir, that my trust in you, and this good lady's earlier defence of you, was not misplaced, and that you indeed had no thought of malice in your heart and mind when the police discovered you inside the church with that other chap.'

'Blimey, guv, I was tryin' to *stop* 'im

from doin' something wicked! Why would I help some gallopin' git take a ruddy great paddy to the haircut?'

For that exchange, I confess Harry lost me right after 'wicked', though the inspector seemed to understand every word. His smile widened and he said, 'The passion of your denial speaks volumes, sir. I am satisfied. But why do you suppose the other fellow would be attempting to desecrate the tomb?'

'He's a nutter, that's why,' Harry said. 'He thought someone else was buried there.'

'The local force has identified this so-called 'nutter' as one Graham Chelish.' Turning his gaze toward me, he added, 'An acquaintance of yours, I believe, Mrs. Watson; a fact you failed to reveal to me earlier.'

'Because 'acquaintance' is perhaps too strong a word,' I replied. 'I have really only met him.'

Inspector Islington's mouth stretched into a smile, but unlike his earlier expressions, this one conveyed no mirth whatsoever. 'He is the husband of the woman you came to Stratford to see.'

'He is, but I only came to try and help solve his disappearance. I knew nothing of his mental instability.'

'I also recall from our earlier conversation, you said that the matter with your friend's sister had no bearing in the case of Professor Macnee.'

'I spoke accurately. It does not.'

'Yet he and Mr. Benbow were found together by the police, and Mr. Benbow has bearing in the case of Professor Macnee, given his participation in the lecture at Madame Tussaud's. It would seem that we are at the crossroads at which all of our disparate paths meet.'

'Except for the one that leads to Oxford,' I said.

'Oxford, dear lady?'

'Graham Chelish was apparently in Oxford researching a book he is writing on Shakespeare. His peculiar behavior in Holy Trinity Church may or may not be related to his research.'

'Do you think you could arrange for me to speak with Mr. Chelish?' the inspector asked.

'I could take you to his house, but I cannot guarantee his condition,' I told him. 'Neither can I guarantee that his wife will allow you to speak with him, particularly if he is agitated.'

'Even so, your offer to introduce us is most gratefully accepted.'

With a sigh I set out for the Chelish home, with the inspector and Harry in tow, though on the way a thought struck me. 'You know, Harry, it may not be the best idea for you to confront Mr. Chelish, given the incident at the church.'

'Oh, right you are, ducks. If it's all right with the guv'nor, I'll be off, then. As long as I'm here, there's a place I want to see with me own eyes.'

'By all means,' the inspector said.

'See you back at the hotel, Amelia,' Harry said. He then scampered down the street like a rabbit.

'You are quite right, dear lady,' Inspector Islington said, watching him go. 'He is a singular fellow.'

When we arrived at Bull Street I was gratified to see that there were no policemen hovering about outside the

Chelish residence. Knocking briskly on the door, I waited for Mary to answer it, which she did cautiously until she recognized me. 'Oh, it is you, Amelia,' she sighed, swinging the door open, but appearing to freeze in place upon seeing Inspector Islington. 'Who are you?'

I introduced the inspector and Mary cried: 'Scotland Yard! What has Gray done now?'

'Please do not alarm yourself, madam,' the inspector said soothingly. 'Your husband is in no trouble. I am following up on a matter that took place in London, for which Mrs. Watson was a witness. It involved a Shakespearean scholar. Mrs. Watson happened to mention that your husband was researching a book in the Shakespearean field, so I am hoping he will be able to answer a few scholarly questions for me.'

That was at least within the same county as the truth.

'I will see if he is awake,' Mary said, disappearing from the sitting room. A few moments later a scream rent the air. Inspector Islington, for all his doughy heft, moved like a deer to the door of the bedroom. I followed, arriving in time to see the distraught figure of Mary Chelish emerging from the darkened room.

'What is it? What is wrong?'

'He's not moving . . . not breathing . . . Gray is dead!'

Fighting numbness, I went into the kitchen and set a kettle of water aboil in order to make a pot of tea, then rushed back to Mary while Inspector Islington examined the late Graham Chelish. Emerging from the room, he announced: 'I can find no pulse. I am so very sorry, Mrs. Chelish.'

'After everything I have been through with Gray, and now this,' Mary said, supporting her face in her hands. 'I dared to believe that he would recover. He was so calm after John returned and gave him that draught.'

'John?' Inspector Islington said. 'Who is John, and what is this draught of which we speak?'

Before I could stop her, Mary said, 'John is Amelia's husband, Dr. John H. Watson, and he came down with her. I asked if he could procure a sleeping draught from the chemist for Gray, and he did, but now . . . ' Her voice trailed off, taking my credibility with it.

'Indeed?' the inspector said. 'Where is the good doctor now?'

'He left, right after administering the medicine.'

Inspector Islington turned his gaze to me. 'Dear lady, it appears that you also failed to tell me that your husband accompanied you to Stratford.'

I sighed, the combined weight of my prevarications suddenly bearing down upon me. 'Mary,' I began, 'there is something you must know. I shall never forgive myself for the duplicity with which I have burdened you. I cannot tell you how sorry I am for my stupid actions, Mary, and to you, Inspector, for deceiving you.'

'Perhaps elucidating them would be more valuable than criticizing them, dear lady,' he said.

Taking a deep breath, I said, 'The man who introduced himself to you as Dr. Watson was not a doctor. Neither was he my husband.'

Mary's reddened eyes grew wide and

fearful. 'I . . . do not . . . understand . . . '

'His name is Gordon Plummer and he is a private investigator.'

'Ahhh, the *dramatis personae* is now complete,' the inspector uttered.

Mary groped for words. 'Why . . . how . . . ?'

'When he introduced himself as John I was outraged, but I foolishly chose not to reveal his lie. I played along, Mary, and I regret doing so with all my heart.'

'Then why did you?'

'It sounds so preposterous now, but you seemed so distressed by Graham's absence, and so relieved that we had come to try and help you, I felt that if we revealed ourselves to be prevaricators from the outset you would not trust us. Or rather trust me, since I am not certain I can trust Mr. Plummer.'

'My god,' Mary whispered, 'you let someone you knew was not a physician administer a drug to my husband? A drug that killed him?'

'Now, now, my good woman, we do not know that for a fact,' the inspector said soothingly. 'Let us keep our heads in this matter. The important thing is that we locate the ersatz Dr. Watson and discover exactly what it was he administered. It is entirely possible that in your husband's agitated state his heart simply gave out, and the drug had nothing to do with it.'

'He has never had a problem with his heart,' Mary replied. 'In fact, in his youth Gray was something of an athlete. His mind may have been faltering, but his body was not.'

'Wait a minute, Mary,' I dared to say. 'The draught would have to have been mixed with water. If the glass is still in the room, perhaps we could find traces of the substance.'

'The doctor . . . or Plummer . . . or whoever he is . . . carried the glass out with him,' she said dejectedly. 'I have already rinsed it.'

There went my only hope of redeeming myself.

'We shall get to the bottom of this,' the inspector said, a bit theatrically I thought. 'For the nonce, I shall go and notify the local police. My most heartfelt condolences, madam.' The inspector bowed slightly and then quickly made his way out of the house.

Turning to Mary and taking her hands, which were limp and cold, I said, 'I assure you, Mary, I had absolutely no intention of causing you or Graham harm of any kind. My foolishness may be indefensible, but my intentions were pure. I pray you will forgive me.'

'I am not angry with you,' she said, sinking onto the settee as though deflating. 'God help me, Amelia, but this might actually be for the best.' Her face was so nakedly vulnerable as she said that, as though the top layer of her skin had turned transparent, revealing only the raw, anguished emotion beneath. My heart nearly broke to see her. 'Am I condemning my soul for saying that?'

I sank down on the sofa myself. 'If you wish me to leave and go back to London, Mary, I will understand. All I seem to have done is make matters worse for you.'

'No, Amelia, don't go. Stay at least for a while. None of this has been your fault.'

I wished I could believe that, but the fact was that I had been the one who brought Gordon Plummer into this house. I began to shiver involuntarily as I realized that both Professor Macnee and Graham Chelish, each a Shakespearean scholar, had been in the company of Gordon Plummer, who in both instances had been pretending to be someone he was not. While I had no evidence that Mr. Plummer — if that was indeed his true identity — was the direct cause of the two deaths, neither did I put much stake in coincidence.

'Amelia, I hope you are not becoming ill as well,' Mary Chelish was saying.

'Hmmm?'

'For a moment you seemed to disappear.'

'I am sorry, Mary. I was lost in thought. Would it be all right if I looked in on Graham?'

Mary looked momentarily puzzled, but then shrugged. 'I suppose so, if you like. He is not in a position to complain.'

While peering at dead bodies was not among my favorite pastimes, my intuition argued that I needed to see things for myself. I tiptoed to the bedroom door and gently opened it.

Graham Chelish's face was covered by the blanket — the work of Inspector Islington, no doubt — though his right arm was protruding from the cover. I stepped over and gently touched his wrist, which was indeed cold. There was no evidence of a pulse. Very carefully lifting the blanket and peering under, I saw that he was still dressed, except for his jacket. On his face was a placid, peaceful expression, as though he were merely sleeping. There was no sign of violence of any kind.

Setting the blanket back down, I started to look around the room, which was scrupulously neat and tidy. I did not know exactly what I was hoping to find until I found it: a small paper packet that had been ripped open and discarded on the floor, having missed a waste basket. I picked it up and examined it, finding traces of a white powder inside. Bringing a tiny sample of it to my tongue with my finger resulted in a familiar taste. I had no idea what had caused the death of Mary's husband, but at least I knew what had not.

After scanning the room a few more times, I exited, leaving Graham Chelish to his not-quite-final resting place and went back to Mary. 'You may be relieved to know,' I began, 'that Mr. Plummer is, in the parlance of the penny dreadful, off the hook, at least in terms of suspicion of poisoning or overdosing. I found the remnants of what he brought back from the chemist. It is plain bicarbonate of soda.'

'Are you certain?'

'Fairly certain, yes. Here is the packet in which it arrived.'

'How odd, then, that it should have had such a calming effect on Graham.'

'Do you know what a placebo is?' Mary shook her head. 'It is an ineffective medicine that nonetheless has curative power, simply because the patient believes it does. Particularly a patient with, forgive me, Mary, a troubled mind.'

'How odd that a man merely pretending to be a physician knew that this . . . whatever you called it . . . would work.'

More likely it was the only substance

he could talk the chemist out of, I thought, but chose not to share that supposition.

A knock came to Mary's door, and it turned out to be a gaggle of policemen come to remove the body in the bedroom, which they did post-haste. Graham was to be transported to the morgue, where he would lie while Mary arranged for burial. 'Surely you are going to do a postmortem examination,' I said.

'We'll arrange for a physician, ma'am,' one officer said as they left with the lifeless form on a stretcher. The door slammed behind them with a note of sepulchral finality, and once more, Mary grew weak. I helped her to the chaise and asked what I could do for her, to try and make up for my blunders heretofore.

'I know I asked you to stay, Amelia, but for the moment I believe what I need most is to be alone for a time, just long enough to collect my thoughts.'

'I understand, dear,' I said, rising.

'But do come back, please.'

Even though she did not say as much, I could see that what she needed was private time to grieve, out of the watchful view of others.

'I will let myself out; but do not worry, Mary — I will come back to check in on you later.'

Wandering about the streets of Stratford until something further happened did not seem like a viable option. I could always return to the Tudor Rose, though there was little to do there except bide my time while waiting for Mr. Plummer or Harry to return. But waiting patiently has never been high on my list of natural abilities. If only I knew where Harry had skipped off to, I could meet up with him and perhaps the two of us could occupy our time visiting the town's historical buildings and sites together. But he had been in such a hurry to get away, and by now he could be anywhere.

'Oh, no, not *anywhere*,' I said aloud, laughing, for I had just realized the likeliest place in Stratford-upon-Avon for Harry to have gone.

11

The Black Bittern, also known as 'the Filthy Fowl', was located at the southern curve of the River Avon, not far from Holy Trinity Church and the Shakespeare Memorial Theatre. I stood at the front door of the establishment, hesitating before entering. While I would have put a wager down that Harry was inside at this moment, I was also a respectable lady from London whose solitary presence in a public house in the afternoon could be considered untoward. My indecision must have been palpable, for a voice behind me asked: 'Are you awaiting someone's emergence, or were you planning on going in?'

I turned to see a man of roughly my age, tall and lean, bespectacled, and with a great shock of grey-brown hair that sat atop his head like the cap of a mushroom. He smiled amiably.

'Oh, I am sorry if I am in your way,' I responded, stepping back.

'If you are deliberating over entering, I can assure you the Fowl is a respectable establishment — except, perhaps for the presence of actors.'

'You do not like actors?' I asked.

'On the contrary, I am devoted to them. I was merely attempting humor. I have the honor of being both dramaturge and resident authority on the works of the Bard for the Memorial Theatre. My name is Morland Greaves.'

This must be the man of whom Mary had spoken; the one who had fallen out with Graham. 'Mr. Greaves,' I said, 'I have heard of you and should like very much to speak with you, sir. Would you think it presumptuous of me if I asked to join you?'

He regarded me with a quizzical look, and then whispered: 'Do forgive me, madam, but you are not . . . I mean, this is not a . . . um, well, a professional proposition is it?'

'Most decidedly not!' I declared. Then I began to laugh. I would have felt more indignant had I not myself worried about my presence here being misinterpreted. 'I know this must seem awkward, but I have a problem on my hands that an expert on Shakespeare may be able to help solve. Your name was given to me as a possible aid.'

'Really? How delightful. Very well, then, I would be honored if you would join me, Miss, uh . . .'

'Mrs. Amelia Watson,' I replied. 'I am here from London.'

Together we entered the so-called Filthy Fowl, whose primary foulness was the cloud of tobacco smoke that all but obscured the ceiling. It was a rather close establishment whose panelled walls were covered with paintings, drawings, and an occasional photograph of players costumed and made up for their Shakespearean roles. Pulling out my handkerchief, I placed it over my face; for his part Mr. Greaves did not notice. He was instead being greeted as a familiar sight by the publican and several of the men at the bar. 'Oy, Morland!' the barkeep called. 'The usual?'

'Perhaps not,' he called back, 'for I have a guest today.'

We settled at a small round table that

was tucked into a corner and was relatively free of the miasmic smoke layer that hung tangibly in the air. A waitress quickly appeared and Mr. Greaves ordered a pint of porter. Since I had managed to miss lunch, I ordered a game pie and a coffee. After our order had been taken, I looked around the establishment to find Harry; to my surprise, he was nowhere to be seen. Perhaps I did not know him as well as I thought. When our order was delivered to our table, I saw with mild distress that my pie was served with mushy peas, a dish I strenuously strive to avoid looking at, let alone consume. My disgust must have shown, for Mr. Greaves said, 'You can send the pie back, if you like.'

'Oh, no, it isn't the pie,' I explained, 'rather the peas. I was not expecting them.' I took a bite of the game pie, concluding that the game in question was guessing what sort of animal was cooked inside. It was edible, albeit barely.

'Now then, Mrs. Watson,' Morland Greaves said, 'you stated there was some matter in which I might be able to provide assistance.'

'It involves the sister of an old friend of mine, Mary Chelish, whose husband Graham — '

'Oh, no!' Mr. Greaves interrupted. 'Not Graham Chelish! Madam, I have nothing against you. You seem like a fine person. But if Chelish has sent you here on his behalf in order to try and persuade me to open up my files to him and support his ludicrous theory, then I must perforce stop this conversation right now.'

'He has not sent me,' I replied, a bit taken aback by his sudden outburst, 'nor could he. He has died.'

'Oh. Oh, dear. I suppose I am sorry, then. I did not wish to speak ill of the dead.' He raised his glass and said, 'To Chelish, may he rest in peace. What is . . . or was, I suppose . . . your connection with the man?'

'It is a long story,' I began, and then tried to state it as briefly as possible, adding: 'Graham's death seems to have put an end to the matter, though I promised to stay a while longer to help Mary through the ordeal. She is quite distressed by the recent inexplicable actions of her husband, which culminated with an attempt to break into the grave of Shakespeare.'

'Oh, dear god!'

'What was it he wanted of you?'

Mr. Greaves sighed. 'He wished me to corroborate an insane theory of his regarding Shakespeare. You may not know it, but there are people out there who have nothing better to do with their time than speculate that the works of William Shakespeare were written by someone else. The root of that presumption is the belief that no bumpkin born in a market town and lacking a university education could possibly be intelligent or talented enough to be Shakespeare. That bit of snobbery was first put forth during Shakespeare's life by a playwright named Robert Greene, who at least allowed Shakespeare was the author. Others since then have started with the conclusion that Shakespeare was simply a mask for another genius, and then set about trying to figure out who it was. First it was Marlowe, then it was Bacon, then Sir Walter Raleigh, then Stanley, and then anyone of note who was a contemporary of Shakespeare's and university educated. Chelish's theory, however, took the prize. I had no patience for it, and told him so in so many words.'

'Was it Queen Elizabeth, by any chance?' I asked.

'The Queen herself? Dear god, no. That is one personage whose culpability I've not heard that put forth as of yet, though I've no doubt that someone, somewhere has come up with it.'

If only you knew, I thought.

'No, Mrs. Watson,' Mr. Greaves went on, 'Chelish's candidate for England's premiere poet was none other than Spain's premiere writer, Miguel de Cervantes Saavedra.'

'The author of *Don Quixote*?'

'Precisely. He had visited me on several occasions, each time becoming more vehement about his theory than the last. Finally I forbade him from coming.'

'When was that?'

'I don't know; three weeks ago, perhaps.'

Shortly before Graham disappeared, in other words. Could whatever altercation had happened between himself and Mr.

Greaves have been the thing that sent him off on his mysterious quest to Oxford?

'Did he ever explain what was behind his bizarre theory?'

'Oh, yes. Have you ever heard of the play *Cardenio*?'

I shook my head.

'At present it is a lost work, but its existence is recorded in history. It has been attributed, at least in part, to Shakespeare. It is said to have been based on both a character and an episode from *Don Quixote*, which is a reasonable assessment, since the play's recorded co-author, John Fletcher, was also known to borrow from the works of Cervantes.'

'Does that not argue instead that Fletcher and Cervantes were one and the same?' I offered.

'On the surface of it, perhaps, though Fletcher is someone we know a little more about. Fletcher was university educated, and his father was known at the court, and it is highly possible that he could have been fluent in Spanish, Latin, and any other number of languages. What he was not fluent in was genius, as were both

Shakespeare and Cervantes. But Chelish thought he had uncovered a piece of evidence so solid that it would brook no argument. Unfortunately, he was quite, quite wrong.'

'What evidence?' I asked.

'History records that both William Shakespeare and Miguel de Cervantes died on the same day: April 23, 1616. On the surface of it, it appears to be quite a coincidence — almost too much of a coincidence. Those with more imagination than knowledge might even infer that the only explanation for the coincidence is that they were one and the same. There is, however, a pesky little problem with that theory.'

I was about to ask for an explanation to his last comment, but was distracted by a loud and boisterous conversation that suddenly emerged from behind me. I turned to see a collection of men emerging from what was apparently a side room to the establishment. 'Glad you're still here, Morland,' one of them called out to Mr. Greaves. 'There's a chap here you'd be interested in talking to.'

'Indeed?' he replied. Then turning to me, he explained, 'These are some of our actors from the theatre, on break from rehearsal and searching for additional talent at the bottom of a pint glass. Please excuse me for a moment.' Standing up to greet the young and rather swaggering fellow who was the head of the group, Mr. Greaves said, 'So, Richard, have you been regaling yet another victim with tales of your triumphs on the stage?'

'Quite the contrary, you emaciated bookworm,' the red-faced man identified as Richard replied cheerfully to the amusement of the men behind, as Mr. Greaves rolled his eyes with comic indignation. I gathered that this was merely an example of the normal banter between them. 'This time we have been listening to a grand fellow who hails from London. His stories of working with Tree and Irving are amazing!'

'Here he comes now!' another of the actors cried, and the group parted to reveal a figure walking in from the back room; a figure whose confident stride and air of authority belied his small stature.

'Morland,' Richard said, 'I would like to introduce you to Mr. Hathaway Broughton, actor extraordinaire.'

Oh, heavens! I thought. My assumption of Harry's whereabouts had been correct after all.

'How d'you do, sir,' Harry said in a plummy voice as he extended his hand toward Morland Greaves, his face an affected mask of blasé diffidence.

'A pleasure, sir,' Mr. Greaves replied, and then he turned in my direction. For a fleeting moment, I thought of simply rising and fleeing, but that would have appeared even more awkward than facing Harry directly. 'I have also made the acquaintance of a visitor from London.'

His nose appropriately elevated to suit his character, Harry turned in my direction, and upon seeing me the lids of his narrowly slitted eyes flew open like window shades. He coughed in order to cover a gasp (which no one but I correctly interpreted), and then in the next instant recovered and resumed his persona as a renowned thespian and leading light of the London stage.

'Gentlemen,' Mr. Greaves went on, 'this lady is Mrs. Amelia Watson, with whom I have just spent a delightful . . .' In one fluid, almost musical sweep, he pulled a watch from his pocket, snapped it open, glanced at it, closed it and replaced it before finishing, ' . . . twenty-six minutes. For those of you who are still sober enough to translate audible sounds into cogent thought, I entreat you to control your language around her.'

'Charmed, I'm sure,' I said. 'And if I am not mistaken, Mr. Broughton, I believe I have seen you act before. Quite recently, in fact.'

'Have you now?' he said uncertainly. 'Well, then, I . . . um, Mr. Greaves, the lads here said I might be allowed to watch them rehearse.'

'I suppose that would be all right,' Mr. Greaves said, 'as long as you do not tread on the toes of our director, Mr. Warbeck.'

Mr. Greaves rose and laid a banknote on the table for his ale and my pie, which I felt was quite generous, and led the small army of theatre people out of the public house. As we walked out, I asked

Mr. Greaves, 'Might I trouble you by posing a few more questions about our mutual friend, Mr. Chelish?'

'No trouble at all, Mrs. Watson. You may join me in my office if you like.'

When we arrived at the Memorial Theatre, the acting contingent veered off toward the rotunda, which was presumably the wing containing the stage. I followed Mr. Greaves through the smaller side building, which was connected by an aerial walkway, and which housed the museum and library, his office being located in the latter. It was a tiny room that was absolutely crammed with books and papers, a pile of which he had to remove from an ancient chair in order to allow me seating. Mr. Greaves took his seat behind his desk, which was similarly buried under towers of books and heaps of paperwork.

'Before we talk about the unfortunate Mr. Chelish,' I began, 'you must tell me about that pesky little fact that belied the common death dates of Shakespeare and Cervantes.'

'Oh, yes,' he said. 'Well, what is that old

adage? 'The devil is in the detail.' In this instance, the elusive detail is that Shakespeare died in England, and Cervantes in Spain, and in 1616 — '

'The two countries were under different calendars!' I blurted out.

'Precisely, Mrs. Watson. Spain had already adopted the Gregorian calendar, but England remained on the Julian calendar until the Georgian era. So even if both died on April 23, it was their respective countries' April 23, some eleven days apart. Chelish, however, rejected that simple fact as an attempt to confuse him. You know, I am not particularly surprised that he attempted to break into the grave of Shakespeare. Actually, it fits rather well.'

'Fits with what?' I asked. 'What could he be hoping to find in the grave?'

'While we know more about Cervantes than we do about Shakespeare, there is one thing that nobody knows: the location of his final resting place. Based upon what you have told me and what I learned firsthand from my dealings with Chelish, it is possible he hoped to prove that the body in the grave of William Shakespeare was in fact that of Miguel de Cervantes Savaadra.' After laughing heartily, Morland Greaves added, 'Can you *imagine* the scandal that would produce?'

12

I confess that I sat there in stunned silence for a few moments. It would require a mind as twisted as that of Don Quixote himself to actually believe that the person in Shakesepeare's grave was Cervantes. Finally, I asked: 'How could Graham have possibly believed he would actually get away with disinterring the body? And providing he managed, how could he have proven who it was? To my knowledge, bones do not speak in their native language.'

'I wonder if perhaps disinterring the body was not really his aim,' Morland Greaves said.

'The police caught him there, tools in hand, or at least in proximity.'

'Exactly. They caught him there. I wonder if perhaps being caught was his objective. You see, he was prevented from opening the grave to ostensibly prove that the world was a victim of a centuries-old conspiracy to obfuscate the truth. To the mind of a crackpot . . . I am sorry, I vowed not to speak ill of him . . . let's say to the mind of someone who believes they alone know the truth, being prevented from proving his theory would confirm that the establishment was conspiring to silence him. That is often all the proof a crack . . . I mean such a person needs to make his case. The truth is, Mrs. Watson, he attempted a similar ruse with me. The last time I saw the man, he attempted to steal some documents from this very room. Fortunately, I was able to prevent him and eject him from the building, but he responded by claiming that I was slandering him because he knew the 'truth' about Shakespeare, a 'truth' I refused to acknowledge.'

'Oh, dear. Well, Mr. Greaves, I shall be no more of a burden to you today,' I said, rising. 'Thank you for your time.'

'It has hardly been a burden, Mrs. Watson.'

I started to take my leave when another question struck me. 'Mr. Greaves, before I go, there is another small puzzle that you may be able to clear up. When the police discovered Graham in the church, I was told he blurted something out, possibly a quote. It had something to do with a foul fiend. I thought it might possibly be from *Mac* ... that is, the Scottish play.'

Morland Greaves rose from his chair and declaimed, ''Away! The foul fiend follows me! Through the sharp hawthorn blows the cold wind. Hum! Go to thy cold bed and warm thee.'' While his recitation was performed with great gusto, he had little natural ability for acting. 'It is not from the Glamis comedy, Mrs. Watson,' he said in his normal voice, 'but rather *King Lear*. It is a line of Edgar's.'

'I wonder why Graham chose that particular line.'

'If you know the play, Mrs. Watson, Edgar is similarly seen as a victim of a continuing conspiracy. Perhaps Chelish identified.'

I started to leave again, but this time was stopped by the sound of angry footfalls coming down the hallway outside; a moment later a man burst into the office as unexpectedly as the jester of a jack-in-the-box. 'Greaves!' the man shouted, rushing past me as though I were not there and striding up to the desk. 'This is the last straw!'

'What is it now, Trevor?' Mr. Greaves sighed.

'Should the time come when I require the services of an assistant, I will sodding well choose the man myself!'

'Trevor, please. We have a guest. This is Mrs. Amelia Watson of London. Mrs. Watson, this is Trevor Warbeck, our director.'

The small, tense figure of Trevor Warbeck glanced back in my direction and said, 'You're too tall. Sorry.'

'I beg your pardon?' I said.

'You're too tall. Even on a raked stage you'd stand out like the spire of Salisbury Cathedral!'

'She is not here to audition, Trevor,' Mr. Greaves said.

'Oh. In that case, how do you do, madam?'

'Fine, thank you,' I said coolly, 'though a bit disconcerted to learn that I belong in a circus freak show.'

'Don't take it personally,' Warbeck snapped. Then he turned to Mr. Greaves and continued his tirade. 'As for you, at the very least you could have warned me that you were going to install a shadow to sit there and pass judgment on every bloody note I give!'

'Trevor, I have not the faintest idea what you are talking about.'

'That man, that Broughton blighter!'

Oh, dear. Clearly toes had been trodden upon.

'Please calm down, Trevor,' Mr. Greaves said. 'Mr. Broughton is an actor from London. I told him that he could watch rehearsal, but I specifically instructed that he should not interfere.'

'Oh, oh, he is not interfering. He is bloody well taking over!'

Oh, dear.

'Come down to the theatre, I'll show you!' Trevor Warbeck cried, and with a sign of resignation, Mr. Greaves stepped around his desk and followed the director out of the office. Sensing that I was already forgotten in the wake of this new problem, I trailed along behind.

'This London jackanapes is turning my rehearsal into a shambles,' Warbeck fumed as we progressed through a series of hallways and staircases. 'He's had the actors practising the finer points of *commedia* slapstick until they were useless with laughter!'

'Would not a little humour make for an entertaining production?' I offered cautiously.

Mr. Warbeck stopped and turned to face me, his eyes daggers. 'Who are you again, madam?'

'Mrs. Amelia Watson,' I told him.

'Yes, well, a little humour might, perhaps enhance the production were we rehearsing *A Comedy of Errors*, Mrs. Watson, but slapstick is a bit out of place in *Julius Caesar*.'

'Oh.'

Ere long we came to the lobby area of a playhouse and, following Mr. Warbeck (who was now moving with the speed and determination of a locomotive, and emitting nearly as much steam), we entered theatre itself.

I was rather taken aback at how small

the Shakespeare Memorial Theatre was. Its gracefully curved lyre-shaped loge hovered over the intimate orchestra section, which in turn gave way to an ample music pit beneath the proscenium stage. On the stage was a group of madly cavorting actors, one of whom was, of course, Harry Benbow. Harry was standing centre stage behind a figure lying on a bier, covered with a sheet. This figure could have easily been mistaken for a cadaver if not for the fact that he was shaking with mirth under the cloth.

'Here is himself, marr'd, as you see, with traitors,' Harry declared over the body. 'So come on, boyos, roll up an' have a butcher's!'

At that the figure under the sheet began to slowly sit up.

'Blimey, not you, Julie!' Harry cried, pushing him back down to the bier as the other actors collapsed in hilarity. 'Brutus, give 'im another one — I think you mucked the job!'

'*Cease!*' Trevor Warbeck shouted in a voice that nearly lifted the roof from the building. How such a voice could have emanated from such a compact figure was a mystery. Casting a lethal finger at Harry, he cried: 'You! Leave this place at once; for if you do not, I will!'

'Trevor, please, calm yourself,' Mr. Greaves was saying, while onstage one of the actors called back: 'We're just having a bit of fun up here, Mr. Warbeck.'

'*Fun?*' the director thundered. 'We are not here to have fun! We are here to create theatrical art! Do I need to say it again?'

'Might want to, guv,' Harry replied. 'I don't think they heard you in Moscow.'

The actors on the stage made valiant but unsuccessful attempts not to laugh at that, as, unless I am very mistaken, did Morland Greaves, who covered his grin with his hand.

'Thank you for coming, Mr. Broughton,' the dramaturge called out once he had recovered. 'Allow me to show you out. The rest of you, carry on, please.'

At the front entrance, Mr. Greaves said, 'It has been a pleasure to meet you both. And do not concern yourself regarding Mr. Warbeck's tantrum; it shall pass. I daresay, Mr. Broughton, that you have done more to boost the morale of the company than an increase in salary.'

Harry puffed up with pride at that.

'But you did not hear that from me,' Mr. Greaves went on. Turning to me, he added, 'Please convey my condolences to Chelish's wife, Mrs. Watson. Goodbye.' The door rapidly closed.

'*Gor*, did you hear that, ducks? The boyos liked ol' Harry's antics more than a fiver! But what was that about condolences? Who up and battered?'

'Battered?'

'Battered an' fried . . . died,' he said. 'I made that 'un meself.'

'Mary's husband, Graham Chelish died today,' I said.

'*Gor*, sorry, Amelia. He weren't murdered, was he?'

'I fervently hope not, Harry.'

We walked in silence for another minute until Harry stopped, suddenly rapt with a sight in front of us. 'Blimey, wouldja look at that.' We were at the edge of a neatly kept garden right on the bank of the river, where a stone bridge crossed it; in the middle of the garden was a large stone pedestal atop of which was a bronze seated figure of William Shakespeare, peering down at the world with a somewhat impatient expression as though anxiously awaiting his cue to enter. 'It's himself,' Harry said reverently.

'It's a statue, nothing more,' I replied. There were other statues surrounding the pedestal as well, representing Falstaff, Lady Macbeth, Prince Hal, and Hamlet.

'Statue or not, it makes me weak in the knees just lookin' at him, and it's like he's lookin' right back at me. Blimey, he don't look none too happy, though. Maybe his ghost don't like what I did to Caesar back there after all.'

'Surely one more unkind cut would not hurt,' a voice directly behind us said, causing poor Harry nearly to jump out of his shoes.

'Gor, did it speak?'

'No, Harry,' I said, turning to face the man behind us. 'Are there three of you, Inspector?' I asked. 'Quadruplets, perhaps?'

'Hardly, Mrs. Watson,' Inspector Islington said. 'How are you, Mr. Benbow?'

'Right enough.'

'I am sorry if I have once again startled you. I merely wished to inquire after the widow Chelish. How is she doing, Mrs. Watson?'

'As well as can be expected. I fear it will take her some time to become used to the idea of her husband's not being there.'

'I do daresay. Dear lady, would you consider it unseemly if I made a small request of you?'

'I would not consider it unseemly of you to ask, as long as you do not consider it unseemly of me to decline your request, should I so desire.'

'Fair enough,' the inspector said. 'What I am asking of you is to observe Mrs. Chelish and report to me any unusual or untoward occurrences that might happen within the confines of her house. Anything she might say that sounds odd or singular to your ears. Would you be so kind as to do that?'

'You are asking me to spy on a woman I have only recently befriended, a woman who is struggling with the sudden loss of her husband?'

'*Spy*, Mrs. Watson?' The inspector began to laugh heartily. 'Well, not to put too fine a point on it, in a word, yes I am. Does that trouble you?'

'It does not elate me.'

'This sounds like my cue to be runnin' along again,' Harry said. 'I'll let the two o' you conduct business.'

'You're not going back to the Filthy Fowl, are you?' I asked.

'Not as if I has to pay for me own drinks, ducks. Those boyos was kind enough to treat, an' now I got a reputation to keep up. But maybe I'll duck in somewhere else.'

'Stay a moment, Mr. Benbow,' the inspector said, not looking at Harry, but holding a hand up to keep him from moving. 'I may have a request for you as well.'

'I was afraid o' that,' Harry grumbled.

'While it is my charge to find out what is transpiring here in the fair village of Stratford, which I do believe relates back to the murder of the unfortunate Professor Macnee, I cannot, despite your clever witticism, Mrs. Watson, be in multiple places at one time. That is why I have asked you to keep Mrs. Chelish within sight and report to me anything pertinent to the case. Your presence, I believe, will be far less intimidating to her than mine.'

He did have a point. 'Very well, Inspector, I shall do my best.'

'Excellent! Now as to you, Mr. Benbow, I am most anxious to find Gordon Plummer and speak to him. My efforts to locate him have thus far proven futile.'

'Have you tried the Tudor Rose?'

'I enquired there. They have not seen him. That is why I am asking you, sir, to keep your eyes open for him.'

'I s'pose I could do that,' Harry allowed. 'But what do I do if I do see him?'

'Stay with him. He knows you and presumably he trusts you. Do not let him out of your sight and do not let him board a train and leave. I only hope he has not done so already.'

It was indeed possible that Gordon Plummer had left the village, since there appeared to be nothing that would keep him here. To my knowledge he was not even aware of Chelish's death, not being amongst us when the body was discovered. He might have simply gone on and continued his pursuit of the mysterious letter of Professor Macnee.

'If you happen to find Plummer,' the inspector was telling Harry, 'get word to me immediately through police headquarters on Rother Street.'

'I dunno, guv; this is seemin' a little like work. I mean, I don't even know where to start lookin'.'

'Since you have already mentioned the intriguingly named Filthy Fowl, perhaps checking it and the other public houses in the town might be a good start.' Reaching into his coat pocket, Inspector Islington withdrew a small purse from which he procured a new sterling silver crown. 'And since your reputation cannot withstand purchasing your own drinks, consider this a stipend in return for your help.' He handed the coin to Harry.

It was hard to tell which glistened more: the inspector's crown or Harry's face upon receiving it. '*Gor!*' Harry cried, shoving the coin into his pocket. 'Ol' Harry's on the job, guv!' He saluted the inspector before dashing away.

'Do you really think that Mr. Plummer is loitering in a public house?' I asked Inspector Islington.

'One never can tell,' he said. 'The larger point, dear lady, is that I will know, roughly, where to find Mr. Benbow, should I require him. There are not that many public houses in Stratford.'

'May I say, Inspector, that you are a rather devious person?'

He smiled, inscrutably. 'There are those who would say that is one of my better qualities. Now, then, I must be about my own business. I shall be in touch, Mrs. Watson.'

Watching Inspector Islington drift away, I was feeling much less sanguine regarding the inspector's requests than was Harry. There was an aura of mystery about the man, particularly his seeming ability to appear out of thin air like a spectre at a séance. Even so, it would hurt neither Mary nor me to spend more time together. Hopefully it would not be an intrusion for me to return so soon, but I had to believe that the inspector suspected there was some information to be gleaned there, or else he would not have dispatched me to keep an eye on Mary.

Upon arriving at the house, I knocked on the door of the Chelish home, but received no answer. I tried once more; maybe she had gone out. I had turned to leave when I heard a frightened voice from behind the door ask, 'Who is there?'

'Mary, it is Amelia Watson,' I said. 'May I come in?'

'Are you alone?'

'Yes. Is something wrong?'

The door opened quickly and the figure of Mary Chelish that stood on the other side of it was that of a woman etched with terror. 'Good heavens, Mary, *now* what?' I demanded as she ushered me in and then closed and locked the door behind me.

'Something is in the house,' she said.

'You mean someone?'

'I don't know. I've heard noises coming from the bedroom as though Gray was back, looking for something.'

'When did you hear these noises?'

'Not more than an hour ago.'

'Did you investigate?'

She looked at me with a panicked expression. 'No. I cannot bring myself to go in there. What if . . . what if Gray were to be in there?'

'Mary, please take control of yourself. Gray is not coming back. You know that.'

'Then who . . . what . . . was making the noise?'

'I shall find out.'

'Amelia, please, don't . . . '

'You cannot live like this, Mary. If someone has entered your home you need to report it to the police. Stay out here if you like, but I am going to find out what, if anything, is causing your disturbance.'

While Mary stayed back, I marched to the bedroom door and pounded on it loudly and forcefully. 'I am coming in!' I cried, and pushed the door open. I looked around the empty, dark bedroom, and finally focused on the wall opposite. 'Oh, dear,' I uttered, and then called out: 'Mary, you had best come and see this.'

'What is it, Amelia?' Mary said, rushing up behind me.

'Look.' The window opposite the door

to the bedroom was wide open, and a rather chill breeze was blowing in.

'That window was closed when they removed Gray's body,' Mary confirmed. 'I was not imagining things, then. Somebody was in here. But who?'

13

'We should notify the police at once,' I told Mary, 'and they will station a man on watch.'

'I do not want to be under constant watch,' she replied, going to the open window to close and lock it.

'They would not be watching you. They would be watching for whoever broke into your home.'

'But it would feel like it was me.'

'Have you been outside of the house today?'

She shook her head. 'Someone from the church came around earlier to discuss the burial, but I have not left here.'

'Perhaps you should.'

'I do not wish to go out, Amelia.'

'Have you eaten anything today?'

She shook her head. 'So much has happened, and I've not felt hungry.'

'I will fix you something,' I said, marching into her kitchen, where I found little fresh food, but managed to improvise a small meal of canned pea soup, cheese, and bread. After setting the kettle on the stove for tea, I carried the meagre meal back into the living room on a tray.

'Thank you,' Mary said.

'I could hardly sit here and let you starve yourself, Mary.'

She tentatively took a spoonful of the soup and a small bite of cheese, which whetted her appetite. Within minutes all of the food was gone. By then the water had boiled, and I repaired to the kitchen, returning momentarily with a pot of tea and two cups.

'Beth told me you had a gift for friendship, Amelia,' she said tearfully. 'Now I know what she meant.'

'Oh, now,' I murmured, 'anyone would do as much, I'm sure.'

Hoping to redirect the conversation, I said, 'You know, Mary, I really never had the opportunity to know Graham, or even meet him under favourable circumstances. You've told me a little about him, but I'm certain there is much more. What kind of man was he?'

At once her face became a living representation of the comic and tragic masks of theatre, with expressions of sorrow and sadness uneasily co-existing with warmth and happiness. 'When we were first married, Gray was the kindest and most considerate of men,' she began. 'We never had children, so he remained devoted solely to me, or rather to us, to our marriage. Perhaps I became too complacent, began to take him for granted, I don't know, but after a while he began to change. It was subtle at first. He began to worry about money in a way he never had before, which I thought was simply because he believed candles would become obsolete as more people put electricity into their homes. He refused to put it into ours, as an act of defiance, but then began to ignore his business. Perhaps that was also an act of defiance against a changing world. I don't know. All I know is that instead of looking for ways to earn more money, he became cavalier about it, even as he pinched every penny. Then came that book.'

'And you have no idea why he suddenly became so struck with the idea of writing a book?'

'We were married for seventeen years,

and never once in that time did I hear him talk about wanting to be an author until this past year. Then it came over him like an illness, that and his fascination with Shakespeare.'

'He had never been interested in Shakespeare before?'

'The only connection I know of between his family and the local Shakespeare industry came through an uncle, who had something to do with the Memorial Theatre.'

'I don't suppose his uncle is still alive, is he?'

'No. Actually, now that I think back on it, he died right before Gray began to talk about this book. Could that be the connection? Could this book be something that his uncle had been working on, and Gray took it over from him?'

'That might serve as an explanation.'

Mary's face darkened once more, and she appeared troubled over something.

'What is bothering you now, dear?' I asked.

'It's foolish, I know,' she began, 'but what if this book, whatever it is, was cursed? What if anyone who works on it meets an untimely death?'

'Really, Mary.'

'I know, it sounds insane. And yet Gray's uncle dies, and now Gray is dead; and the very day of his death, he was accused of attempting to break into Shakespeare's tomb. Isn't there a curse carved into the gravestone? What if that is not just a poem, but an actual curse?'

'I am sorry, Mary, but I cannot believe in such fantastical rumination, and I suspect that you truly do not either.'

She shuddered. 'I feel as though I am living under a curse.'

I did my best to comfort her, to little avail. Then I had an idea. 'I think a change of scene might do you good, Mary,' I said. 'The situation with Graham would be troubling enough on its own without evidence that someone had broken into the bedroom. Perhaps you need to be away from this house for a while. Why don't you come back to the Tudor Rose with me and stay there tonight.'

She brightened a little. 'You could arrange that?'

'I am certain I could.'

'Thank you. To be honest, I doubt I would be able to sleep in there tonight anyway.' She nodded toward the bedroom.

'It is settled, then. And as for tomorrow, we shall worry about that tomorrow.'

As Mary packed the few items she would need for the evening and next morning, I considered how this arrangement might, in addition to bringing some succour to Mary, actually solve a few other ongoing problems. I would be able to gather some more information about Graham Chelish that might be of use to Inspector Islington, and once Harry was cleared of all complicity in the business at the church, I could put him on the train back to London. Without Harry to worry about, I would be able to more clearly focus my attentions on Mary.

The unknown element remained Gordon Plummer; hopefully Harry had been successful in locating him and delivering him to the inspector.

Once we had arrived at the Tudor Rose, Emrys Price proved only too happy to provide a room for Mary, which was all the way down the hall from my own. Once she had taken stock of it, she followed me to my room, where we sat for the next two hours further familiarizing ourselves with each other and regaling one another with tales of our past, many of which involved our mutual connection, Beth. She said nothing of Graham's death or of what she planned to do with the rest of her life without him. She seemed to want to avoid the topic.

'So tell me, Amelia,' she said, her face taking on the same girlish look I had seen in her sister, 'what is your husband like? I mean your *real* husband.'

I was unable to stifle a chuckle. 'Heavens, Mary, I still cannot believe I allowed that Canadian to lie to you so blatantly. By contrast John is a fine, honest and caring husband, usually.'

'Oh?'

'My husband suffers from an addiction, I'm afraid.'

'Good gracious, Amelia, it is not narcotics, is it?'

'No. It is Sherlock Holmes.'

'Don't you like Sherlock Holmes?' she asked, seemingly startled.

'It is not that I do not like him,' I said, not wishing to complicate the conversation by admitting that we were in truth distantly related, a fact that had been unknown to either of us until a year ago. 'Heaven knows he is not the easiest man with whom to develop a personal relationship, though there are times when I feel rather sorry for him. He has been so alone for so much of his life, except for John. But he is a rather intimidating figure. For the first year or so of my marriage to John, I felt like the wife in a third-rate melodrama whose every action was conducted under the gaze of a sinister ancestor from a portrait that hangs over the hearth, whose eyes never leave you.'

'Oh, I am positively chilled!' Mary said, giggling.

'But I recovered.'

'Bravo!'

We spoke of many other things long into the evening, after I had abandoned all consideration of gleaning information for Inspector Islington. I sensed that

Mary's recent problems had been such that it had been quite some time since she had the opportunity to actually sit with a sympathetic and willing partner and converse. But as night encroached, I felt I had had enough.

'You know, Mary, I am quite exhausted from the day, and I am certain that you could use the rest as well. I fear I must turn in. I will see you in the morning.'

'You are quite right, Amelia. I do need my rest. Good night, and thank you again.'

I walked her to her room, and on the way back knocked on Harry's door, just in case he had managed to slip in. There was no reply. Either he was there, having found Mr. Plummer and reported back to the inspector, and asleep, or he was still out on the town, in which case the next time I saw him I doubted he would be in much of a position to see me back. Not clearly, anyway. Going down and knocking on Mr. Plummer's room brought an equal silence.

To make absolutely certain, I returned to the desk downstairs, behind which

Glynis was seated. 'Have you happened to see Mr. Benbow or Mr. Plummer come in tonight?' I asked.

'I haven't been here that long,' she replied.

'I see.' I turned to go back upstairs, but then felt a slight pang in my stomach, and realized that I had neglected to eat anything since the questionable game pie at the Filthy Fowl that afternoon. Turning back, I said, 'I am sorry to have to ask this, my dear, but would it be possible to get some food here? I'm afraid I've missed dinner.'

Sighing as though the request was the greatest burden of her day, she answered, 'There's some sandwiches in the back. Hold on.' After disappearing into the hotel's kitchen, she returned with a surprisingly tempting-looking ham sandwich.

'Thank you so much, Glynis,' I said, taking it.

'What do you care if Talf goes hungry?' she muttered.

'You know, my dear, while I am most appreciative of your accommodating me with a sandwich, I have not been impressed by your attitude toward the paying customers. I am sorry to be so frank, but if you wish to stay at this job — '

'Who says I want to stay at this job?' she said angrily. 'I'm here because my father made an arrangement with my uncle, but neither of them asked me what I wanted.'

'Oh. Well, I'm sorry. Thank you for the sandwich.'

'Talfryn's going to take me away from all this. You see if he doesn't, no matter what my uncle says.'

'Yes, well, good night.'

I could not help but feel a little sympathy for the girl, despite her rough manners. This was the twentieth century, and women, particularly young women, were still too often relegated to a subservient position to their male counterparts.

Back in my own room I ate the sandwich and set about to free myself from my dress and took down my hair, washed and donned my nightgown. Even though it was not yet ten o'clock, I knew I would have no trouble falling asleep once

I slid in between the sheets.

Staying asleep, alas, would prove to be another matter. I was happily drifting away into dreamless oblivion when an insistent sharp rapping invaded my consciousness. Was it a dream? I hoped so. But it came again, louder this time. In my waking-sleeping disorientation, I imagined it to be Mr. Poe's Raven pounding at my door, until a hissed voice accompanied it: 'Amelia, open the rory!'

'The what?' I managed to say, and it was the sound of my own voice, rather than the rapping, that finally shed off the last coverlet of sleep. 'Good heavens,' I muttered as I got up and stumbled toward the door of the room, opening it a crack. Standing on the other side was the rather flushed face of Harry Benbow. 'Harry, what on earth . . . what time is it?'

'Dunno, but the pubs is closed.'

'Is Mr. Plummer with you?'

'Mr. who?'

'Plummer.'

'Are the pipes clogged?'

'I mean Gordon Plummer!'

'Oh, the canuck? Naw, never set eyes

on 'im. Lessen that's him creepin' around outside with the candle.'

'What did you say, Harry?'

'Some bloke is loiterin' outside the house.'

So I had not been dreaming last night! I really did see someone through the window. 'Wait for me while I get a wrap, Harry.' Going back into the dark room, I felt around until I found my robe, and then went back to the door. Harry was leaning against the jamb, his left coat sleeve sodden with spilt ale. 'You wear your night's festivities on your sleeve, Harry,' I said.

'Huh?'

'Nothing. Come on.' I struggled to keep him upright on the staircase to the ground floor. Neither Emrys Price nor Glynis was anywhere to be seen, though Harry pointed to the window in the darkened day room.

'Right there,' he said.

It took only a second for me to see the tiny point of light made by the flickering candle, which dimly illuminated the man's hand but not his face. Then the light began to move across the side yard until it came into contact with another figure holding another candle! 'There are two of them!' I said. As we watched the candles appeared to pass each other, and then they stopped in place, as though the figures holding them were caught in an embrace.

'Oh, good heavens,' I moaned. 'I should have guessed.'

'Guessed what?' Harry uttered.

'Juliet is meeting Romeo. Go on up to bed, Harry. I believe I can confront our phantoms on my own.'

'You sure, Amelia?'

'I am positive. Lie down and rest your head.'

'Blimey, it needs it,' he said. 'The local ale round here is called Flower's, and now I know why. It gives you a *bloomin'* headache.'

'Good *night*, Harry,' I groaned, pushing him toward the stairs. Since I did not hear the sound of a small body tumbling back down, I had to assume he made it to his room.

Keeping one eye on the figures outside

the window, I waited until he was at the top of the stairs before going out into the still, crisp night. Remaining very quiet, I could hear a whispered conversation coming from the yard. Stealthily I approached, coming close enough to see the two figures faintly illuminated in the moonlight, stopping only when one of them said, 'Shhh! Someone's here!'

'It is Amelia Watson, Glynis,' I announced.

'Mrs. Watson!' she cried, so startled she dropped her candle on the ground. 'Why are you out here?'

'Chasing phantoms, and I assume the phantom with you is named Talfryn.'

'What of it?' a male voice asked.

'It's all right, Talf,' Glynis said. 'She's a guest.'

My eyes had become accustomed to the dark well enough to see that the young man was tall, strapping and handsome in a dark, brooding way.

'You going to report us to my uncle?' Glynis said.

'It is none of my business,' I said, 'unless Talfryn happens to know anything about a break-in that occurred today at the home of Graham and Mary Chelish on Bull Street.'

'I have no idea what you're talking about,' Talfryn replied, stretching the last syllable of *about* twice as long as necessary. The Welsh *about* was easier on the ears than the Canadian *oaut*.

'I don't care if you do tell my uncle about us,' Glynis said defiantly. 'I'm going to escape with Talfryn to someplace no one will ever find us. Come along, Talf.'

'Now?' he asked. 'We're escaping now?'

'We're getting away from *her*,' the girl declared, turning and striding away. Talfryn followed, and I stayed just long enough to see them disappear into the darkness before turning around and heading for the door of the hotel myself.

The scream came before I was even inside.

Turning back, I called out 'Glynis? What is the matter?' My answer was another scream and a shouted oath from Talfryn. Rushing through the darkness, I made my way through the side yard and into the garden, where I once more saw the star-cross'd Welsh lovers, dimly illuminated by the candle. Talfryn was enfolding Glynis protectively in his arms.

'What is it?' I asked, rushing to them.

'Down there,' the young man said, his voice shaky.

Looking down, I saw yet another figure, this one stretched out on the ground, face down. 'Give me the candle,' I demanded, and Talfryn did. Kneeling down, I touched the neck of the prone figure and found it cold as a glacier. With some effort I managed to roll it over and held the light down. 'Dear God,' I uttered, slowly rising.

The figure on the ground was a man; a dead man.

It was Gordon Plummer.

14

It remained oppressively dark outside as we sat in the day room of the Tudor Rose — *we* consisting of myself, Glynis Price, Talfryn Bowen, Emrys Price, several policemen including Constable Constable, and a rather smug-looking inspector named Fox. Both Harry and Mary Chelish were blissfully asleep upstairs, despite the commotion that took place upon finding the body of Mr. Plummer. One did not have to be a trained officer to detect that the Canadian had been stabbed to death, though no trace of any bladed weapon appropriate to the task had been found on the premises.

As far as Mr. Price was concerned, the killer was Talfryn Bowen, since he was the only one whose presence here had not been previously known. Talfryn, of course, loudly proclaimed his innocence, and I, for one, believed him. Any killer who would loiter around the murder scene as if waiting for the body to be found would have to be an idiot. While the rough-hewn young man struck me as impetuous, he did not appear idiotic.

Since I was the only one who knew anything about Mr. Plummer, Inspector Fox spent a good deal of time tapping me for information. In the final accounting, however, there were more questions regarding the dead man than there were answers. 'Has anyone notified Inspector Islington?' I asked the policeman.

'We may only be provincial coppers, madam,' Inspector Fox sneered, 'but I believe we can get to the bottom of this without help from a Londoner.'

'No doubt,' I replied insincerely, 'though I do think he would want to know about this development.'

In the next instant I heard a familiar voice chime, 'Always thinking of others. How gracious of you, Mrs. Watson.'

It was Inspector Islington, appearing as though cued, though whence he materialized at that moment I hadn't a clue. 'Nasty business, this, eh?' he said, suppressing his customary smile.

'Very,' Constable Constable said, only to receive a stern look from Fox for speaking out of turn.

'And I understand you discovered the body, dear lady?' the inspector went on, ignoring the other policemen.

'Not really,' I told him. 'The young lady over there and her gentleman friend actually discovered it, though I suppose you could say I was the first on the scene.'

'What can you tell me about the circumstances of the discovery?'

'Here now!' Inspector Fox cried. 'I'm in charge of this investigation, if you please!'

'Oh, of course, sir, of course,' Inspector Islington said. 'My apologies. Please do carry on.'

Inspector Fox did, but once his attention had turned to Talfryn, Inspector Islington gently took me by the arm and walked me across the room, quietly asking, 'What is your assessment of that young man?'

'Talfryn?' I whispered back. 'I do not believe he knows anything about Mr. Plummer's death, save for the fact that it happened on these premises. I would say the same for Glynis Price.'

'And what of our friend Mr. Benbow?'

'Upstairs, asleep. He was on duty following the trail you provided him access to until closing time.'

'Money well spent, I trust?'

'He never spotted Mr. Plummer.'

'That is, perhaps, because the man was already here in the yard.'

'How could he have been lying here all day without being seen? I am quite positive the side yard was cadaver-free when I arrived back this evening with Mary, so — '

'You mean Mrs. Chelish?' the inspector interrupted.

'Yes. There was evidence that someone had broken into her house, so she did not want to stay there alone. She checked in here. She is asleep upstairs.'

'How utterly interesting,' he mused. 'One body found in her house, and another found mere hours later in the place in which she is staying.'

'Oh really, Inspector, you can't believe that Mary has anything to do with this.'

'I am merely posing an observation,

dear lady. Now, what of this presumed break-in?'

'At her house? I don't know. Mary claimed she heard noises like someone was in the bedroom, and then we discovered the bedroom window open, as though someone had entered and exited.' A thought struck me then. 'It was not you by any chance, was it, Inspector?'

He genuinely seemed surprised. 'I? Why would you think that?'

'I'm merely posing an observation,' I replied. 'Namely, that you have a propensity for appearing out of thin air.'

'Here now,' Inspector Fox's voice called out behind us, 'what are you two going on about over there?'

'Nothing, nothing,' Inspector Islington replied, walking me back into the fray.

'If you are trying to withhold evidence from me, I'll have you both behind bars, London copper or no,' Fox charged.

Inspector Islington's smile became fixed and rather hard. 'You would do well, sir, not to make idle threats.'

'Idle my arse,' Fox said quite ungallantly. 'You've no jurisdiction here.'

'I believe I do, and when the time comes to support my claim with proof, I shall be more than happy to do so. For the time being, however, I suggest you see about having the unfortunate Mr. Plummer removed from the premises and let these good people go about their business. It is clear that no one here committed this heinous murder.'

'Oh, it's clear, is it,' Fox said.

'Quite,' Inspector Islington said. 'I took the liberty of examining the body outside before joining you. Even if the murderer had used a sword, some of the blood that emanated from the wound would have found its way to their clothing. A survey of the assemblage in this room reveals that no one here has a drop of blood on them.'

Instinctively I looked down at my hands to make sure that they had not touched any blood when I turned the body over. Unlike Lady Macbeth, I saw none.

'That's one theory,' Inspector Fox grumbled. 'Okay, right, everybody move on, but don't go far. Once we've finished questioning the people upstairs, we may want to talk with all of you again.'

Having been given leave, I immediately returned to my room and let the police continue their work, though I doubted I was to get any more sleep this night. Rather than court frustration in an attempt to do so, I instead searched for the book I had tucked into my bag in London and commenced reading; though my mind, either through fatigue or over-stimulation, or both, was not in much of a mood to concentrate on the words. Glancing over at the room's bookshelf, I saw a thick volume that, even from this distance, announced itself as *The Complete Works of William Shakespeare*. Getting up and retrieving it, I brought it back to the bed and began flipping through it, stopping when I came to *King Lear*.

As I scanned the pages, growing drowsy, a familiar phrase jumped out at me: *Away! The foul fiend follows me.* 'Oh, of course,' I said, suddenly remembering the scene; it was only one of the most famous of the play, the storm on the heath. Lear, Kent and the Fool encounter Edgar, who is disguised as the lunatic Mad Tom.

Despite my fears that sleep was impossible, at some point in the midst of Act IV I dropped off, awakening several hours later with the book still spread open across my chest. Using the level of daylight coming into the room as a gauge, I guessed it to be between six and seven o'clock. The faint tolling of a church bell a few minutes later confirmed my guess: seven.

Upon descending into the day room after my toilette, I saw that Mary Chelish had already arisen and was finishing a plate of eggs and bacon in the breakfast nook. When she saw me, she flagged me over to the small table and said, 'Amelia, did you hear what happened last night? The police awakened me in the middle of the night to ask some questions. That friend of yours was murdered here!'

'I know,' I replied. 'I was there when the body was discovered. And he was more of an acquaintance than a friend.'

'Still, to be killed like that! That inspector from London asked me about him, but all I knew about him was that he pretended to be your husband.'

Emrys Price came into the dining room wearing a tired, sour expression. 'Will you be wanting breakfast, Mrs. Watson?' he asked.

'One egg, soft-boiled, toast and tea, if you please.'

'Fine. It will take a few minutes as there's but one of me today.'

'One of you? Did something happen to Glynis? Heavens, the police did not arrest her, did they?'

'No, though I almost wish they had,' the man growled.

'Why on earth would you wish that?'

'Because then I'd know where she is. The girl's run off somewhere with *him*.'

'Talfryn? Are you certain?'

'She's not here, and he's nowhere to be seen. So they must be together somewhere. Maybe if the girl gets caught she'll learn to respect her elders.'

'How old is Glynis, Mr. Price?'

'Twenty.'

'Then I would think she is quite old enough to make decisions on her own.'

Emrys Price bowed his head and sighed. 'Try explaining that to my brother

Hugh, the girl's father,' he said.

'Is he really so fearsome?'

'Hughie put up half the money to allow me to open this place, so I definitely owe him. Keeping an eye on Glynis and keeping her away from *him* was part of the debt. Now they're gone and everything's bollixed up.'

'For what it's worth, Mr. Price, I did not get the impression from meeting Talfryn last night that he was a bounder.'

'So where is he?' the man asked, and then repaired to the kitchen without another word.

In light of the situation, it was a valid question. Why *did* Glynis and Talfryn flee the police the first chance they got? Could it be that I was wrong about the characters of one or both of them? I had convinced myself that only the stupidest of killers would remain at the site and wait for the body to be discovered; what if it was in fact only the *cleverest* of killers who would do that?

Whatever Emrys Price might have been thinking about his niece and irate brother, it did not affect his cooking. Within minutes he brought a perfect soft-boiled egg, toast and a pot of tea, and set it all on the table in front of me. Mary returned to her room while I ate, and once I had finished, I started back toward my own. Passing the day room, however, I saw a familiar figure filling the doorway. 'Good morning, Inspector,' I said.

'Good day, good day,' Inspector Islington rejoined. 'I was hoping to find you here.'

'You have some news?'

'About the cases, no. I do, however, concur with your assessments of the young man and young woman. After questioning them thoroughly, I have absolved them of any participation in the unfortunate dispatch of Gordon Plummer. Incidentally, the next time they are seen, I daresay they will be man and wife. The wedding, I believe, will take place in Land's End in Cornwall.'

'You know, Inspector, there are times when I wonder if you are the author of the book in which we are all characters. You seem to know everyone's every move.'

'Were that true, dear lady, Gordon

Plummer would still be alive. Now then, is Mr. Benbow still on the premises?'

'As far as I know he is asleep upstairs.'

'By all outward appearances he is a deep sleeper. We were unable to rouse him during the night, no matter how much we knocked.'

'He was feeling a bit under the table last night, if you know what I mean.'

'I see.'

'I hope you are not still considering Harry a suspect.'

'As to that, let us step back and look at the situation overall. There were three people involved in the lecture given ostensibly by Professor Macnee in London. One was the actual professor, another was the Gordon Plummer in the guise of the professor, and the third was your friend Harry Benbow. Two of them are dead. Does that signify anything to you?'

'I refuse to think Harry had anything to do with those murders!'

'As far as committing them, I agree wholeheartedly,' he said. 'I am more thinking that he may be in danger as well.'

'Oh. Oh dear.'

'You have not seen him this morning?'

'Not since the body was found outside.'

'Perhaps we should endeavour to insist upon entry into his room, then.'

He started for the stairs, and I kept with him, step for step, praying that his suspicions were unfounded. On the first floor we went straight to Harry's room and I rapped gently on the door. Receiving no reply, I rapped more loudly and said, 'Harry, it's Amelia. Please open the door.' This time there was a rustling sound coming from within. A few moments later, the door creaked inward a few inches and there stood Harry Benbow, his hair shaped like a pile of hay through which the wind had blown, having apparently slept in his shirt and trousers. His jacket was carelessly draped over a chair. '*Gor*, Amelia, what time is it?' he asked groggily.

'It is some time after eight. Inspector Islington is here and has requested to see you.'

'Crikey,' he muttered, putting his hands to his head, as he lurched over to the bed and sat on the edge of it.

As Inspector Islington stepped in, his eyes darted across every corner and surface of the room. 'Feeling poorly, Mr. Benbow?' he asked.

'Uneasy lies the head what spent your crown, guv. From now on it's boy's beer for ol' Harry.'

After emitting a small chuckle in response, the inspector said, 'Could you please tell me exactly what you saw when you returned to this establishment last night?'

'Well, I saw someone creepin' around the house through the window downstairs. I came up and rapped up Amelia an' told her, and she said she knew who it was. Least I think she did. Memory's a little faint, if you know what I mean.'

'Could you have seen Plummer at any point and not remember it?'

'Naw, I'd've remembered. Why don't you go ask the ol' boy himself? He must o' come back at some point.'

'He did,' the inspector said, 'though I'm afraid we cannot ask him that or anything else. Mr. Plummer's body was found in the yard outside this house in the middle of the night.'

'Criminee!' Harry said, sliding off the bed and starting to pace. 'He's brown bread, too? Then that must've been him what I saw through the window.'

'No, Harry,' I said, 'it was Glynis Price, the housekeeper, and her gentleman friend. They were secretly meeting outside at night so no one would see.'

'So they took care o' Plummer?'

'They had the misfortune to be the first to stumble over the body,' the inspector said. 'A thorough lack of evidence pointing to their culpability argues for their innocence.'

'Then who d'you think done it?'

Inspector Islington said nothing, but continued to study Harry with a penetrating gaze.

'Oh, now hold on a minute, guv!' Harry cried. 'It weren't me! I might o' killed about a dozen or so pints last night, but no canuck!'

'I am afraid, my good man, that remains to be seen.'

'Just a minute, Inspector,' I cried. 'Downstairs you told me that you thought

Harry might be in danger himself! Now you've changed your mind and you think he's the killer? That's absurd!'

'Downstairs he was not a suspect,' Inspector Islington said. 'But now I have had the opportunity to examine the evidence.'

'What evidence?' Harry and I both shouted in unison.

'Your jacket, sir. That is your jacket hanging on the chair over there, is it not?'

'Yeah, it's mine. What's wrong with it?'

The inspector approached the garment and carefully lifted it off, then walked it over to the window and positioned it under a stream of sunlight. 'What does this look like to you?' he asked, holding out the sleeve of the coat.

'*Gor!*' Harry cried, blanching as he saw the dark red smear on the material.

'Good lord,' I uttered, now seeing that the blotch I had misidentified early in the morning as an ale stain could be only blood.

15

'I dunno how that got there!' Harry cried. 'I din't even notice it till now!'

'It appears to have dried,' the inspector said, carrying the coat to the bed and gingerly draping it over the pillow. 'That would indicate the blood had been there at least overnight. Show me your hands, please.'

'What?'

Instead of asking again, Inspector Islington took Harry's hands forcefully in his own and held them up for examination. He carefully checked both hands, closely examining the fingernails.

'Inspector, please,' I protested, but he ignored me.

'Did you wash these last night?' Islington demanded.

'Yeah, is that against the blinkin' law now?'

The inspector strode to the hand basin on the stand across from the bed, and examined it. 'This is dry,' he said. 'Where's the water?'

'Oh, right, I, uh, well, I emptied the water into the . . . you know, under the bed?'

'The chamber pot?'

'Right.'

Picking up the small white towel on the wash stand, the inspector examined it as well. 'No trace of blood here,' he said.

'That is good news,' I commented.

'It is neither good nor bad. He could have washed all traces off before using the towel and then poured the bloody water into the underbed receptacle, knowing it would make detection that much more difficult, not to mention unsavoury.'

'No, no, that ain't the way it was!' Harry protested.

'Harry, could you have broken a glass and cut yourself last night?' I asked. 'In any of the pubs or taverns you visited, were there any fights? Could the blood have gotten on your jacket that way?'

'No, nothin' like that!'

'Mr. Benbow, the blood has to be there by some fashion,' the inspector charged, 'and with each theory that is denied, only one unpleasant possibility looms on the horizon.'

'Think, Harry,' I commanded. 'Could you have come into contact with Mr. Plummer without realizing it?'

'I ain't sayin' I wasn't right tiddly last night, but I think I'd remember fallin' down on top of a stiff, whether I recognized 'im or not.'

I stared pleadingly at the inspector, who merely shrugged. 'I am sorry, Mr. Benbow, but in light of the evidence on your garment, you will have to accompany me to the Stratford police station.'

'*Gor.* Here we go again.'

'Don't worry, Harry, I will think of something,' I said.

He tried to smile. 'You always do, ducks.' He moved to take up his jacket, but the inspector prevented him.

'My apologies, but I must maintain possession of this coat until the matter is straightened out,' he said, picking it up so as not to disturb the stain.

Harry walked out into the hallway like a man being led to the gallows, with the inspector behind him, and I brought up the rear. As we descended the stairs, I noticed that Harry appeared to be favouring one leg over the other. 'Harry, you are walking as though you are injured,' I said. 'Is something wrong with your leg?'

'Oh, well, it's nothing, ducks,' he replied.

'Mr. Benbow,' the inspector said, 'if there is something you wish to confide, now would be the best time to do so. Otherwise, I may have no other recourse but to assume you were hurt during an altercation with the victim.'

We were at the bottom of the stairs now, and Harry stopped to massage his sore left thigh. 'A what? No, no, it weren't nothin' like that, guv. It's kinda embarrasin', really, but I took a pratter last night in the street comin' back here.'

I had not noticed a limp in the early hours of the morning, but then Harry was so inebriated that his staggering about would have covered it.

'How did you manage that?' I asked, feeling that I knew the answer, having seen his condition.

'Well, this bloke ran smack into me and knocked me down. Didn't even stop to say he was sorry, just kept going. Din't bother me all that much last night, but it's kinda stiffed up on me this mornin', and then comin' down the stairs like that — '

'Someone ran into you?' I cried.

'Yeah. Since I weren't expectin' it, I weren't prepared for the fall. Not like the old days, when I could do a buster on the boards and get right back up.'

'Harry! Why didn't you tell us this before?'

Now the inspector was regarding me with interest.

'I dunno.' Harry shrugged. 'Din't seem important, I guess. And like I said, it was kind of a blow to the ol' dignity.'

'Good heavens, Harry, don't you see what this means? Whoever it was that ran into you could have been the killer fleeing the scene! He could have had blood on *him*, and when he collided with you, some of it might have transferred onto *your* clothing. That could be the source of the blood smear!'

'Crikey, you're right!'

'It is a point worth considering,' Inspector Islington said, bobbing his large head up and down as he pondered it. 'Mr. Benbow, if you could show me where this night-time collision occurred, it would be most helpful.'

'Right-o. Follow me.'

Newly energized, he strode briskly, though still with a limp, out of the rooming house while both Inspector Islington and I struggled to keep up with his pace. At a certain point in the street, Harry stopped and looked around. 'All right,' he began, 'I was comin' from the middle o' town, which is that way. So I was just about here.'

'You are certain of this?' the inspector asked.

'Well, not exactly, but this'd be about right, I think.'

'And whoever it was simply appeared running down the street and collided with you?'

'One minute I'm makin' my way back and the next, *boom*, I'm on me pipe an' drum an' he's runnin' off.'

'Did you see or hear the person running away?'

'Heard him, didn't see him.'

'Then you must have heard his approach as well.'

Harry thought a moment. 'Now that you mention it, guv, there weren't no footsteps before we ran into each other. Why would that be, you s'pose?'

Inspector Islington did not answer. Instead he appeared to be suddenly captivated by a low hedge on the side of the road. Walking over to it, he knelt down and began searching for something. After a few moments, he cried: 'Eureka!' Walking back to us, he held up a knife, which despite the dried blood on the blade, glinted in the sunlight.

'Is that the murder weapon?' I asked.

'Quite possibly,' the inspector answered.

'What's it doin' there, then?' Harry asked.

'Reflect upon it. Why would you have not heard approaching footsteps before you were shoved to the ground? Because the person was not running toward you;

he was already here, waiting to lunge. That hedge is the only place in this immediate area that would offer any kind of cover.'

'All right, but what's he doin' there waitin' for me?'

'Imagine that you are a murderer, and it is the middle of the night. You track your quarry, in this instance, Mr. Plummer, and kill him. Then you attempt to flee the scene, but as you run, you hear the approach of another person, who is now blocking your escape route. That would be you, Mr. Benbow. Our murderer now finds himself trapped. He crouches and hides by the hedge, hoping he will remain unseen. But because of the glow from that street lamp over there, dim though it may be, it remains enough to make total concealment impossible. The killer must therefore take drastic action to prevent discovery. When you get close enough to see him, he lunges out and attacks you, hoping for the element of surprise.'

'He blinkin' well got it,' Harry said.

'Perhaps his intention is to cause you bodily harm, but the collision is forceful enough to knock the knife out of his grasp, sending it flying into the bushes. Or perhaps he tried to hide the knife, or simply dropped it and was unable to find it again in the dark, so that his motive for attack is simply to startle and distract you enough to allow him to escape. In any event, that explains how the blood came to be on your coat.'

'An' you can figger all that out just from me havin' a sore duff?'

'As well as your other testimony. I admit it is largely conjecture, though it is conjecture that happens to fit the facts of the case as are presently known.' Carefully wrapping his newfound prize in a handkerchief, he placed it in his coat pocket and said, 'I would still like you to accompany me to the police station, Mr. Benbow, so that we may get a more complete statement from you.'

'All right, if Amelia comes too.'

'I'll come,' I said.

We walked largely in silence until we came to a small brick building that housed the police headquarters, by which time Harry appeared to have walked out the ache and stiffness in his hip and leg. Entering the building, we proceeded through the less than bustling public area and were, alas, confronted by Inspector Fox.

'Are you making an arrest here?' he demanded.

'I am not,' Inspector Islington answered, 'though I have blood evidence.' He held up the knife. 'Do you have anything for me?'

The Stratford inspector's gaze could have frozen brandy solid. Clearly something had passed between the two police officials that probably had to do with Islington's jurisdiction and status, and Fox was not happy as a result. 'Yeah, I've got something for you, chummy, and this is one you can have all to yourself. I'm interested to hear how a London bloke would handle something like this.' Turning to the hallway, he shouted: 'Muldoon, get in here!' and soon a young officer rushed in. 'Tell the inspector here what you told me.'

'Well, there's a problem at the morgue, sir. The body of the fellow who was stabbed last night was there.'

'Yes, yes, I should think he would be,' Inspector Islington said.

'But that's just it, sir. He was the only one there.'

'I do not follow you, Constable. To my knowledge there was only one knifing victim last night.'

'Well, yes sir, but when we brought Plummer in this morning, the body of that other fellow was already laid out there. Kellish, I think his name was.'

'Chelish,' Inspector Islington corrected. 'Now please get to the point.'

The young constable cleared his throat uncomfortably. 'Yes sir, the point. Well, the point is, now it's only Plummer in there.'

Inspector Islington blinked a few times, and then glared at the young constable. 'Are you saying, Officer, that the body of Graham Chelish has disappeared from the Stratford morgue?'

'Yes, sir. That's the problem I was talking about. He's gone, like he was never there.'

16

'Stealin' a body don't make no sense,' Harry said as the two of us made our way out of the police station, from whence we had virtually been ejected. Harry was still in his shirtsleeves, due to the fact that his jacket was being held as evidence. But at least he was not under arrest.

As for the theft of the body being senseless, I wished I could agree with him. But a terrible black veil of suspicion had fallen over my mind, and I was afraid to admit that I was beginning to suspect someone of being behind all of the deaths and strange occurrences that had taken place over the last two days. It was absurd, of course; but like so many absurdities, it was at least a possibility. I tried to fight the notion, drive it out of my head, but the facts would not allow it to leave. The facts, at least as known by me, all pointed in one direction.

'Harry, I have a terrible feeling I know

who is responsible for the deaths of Mr. Plummer and Graham Chelish.'

'Really? Don't keep me in suspense, Amelia.'

'Mary Chelish.'

'*Gor*, you really think it's yer ol' friend what's done it?'

'Technically, Harry, she is not an old friend. She is the sister of an old friend. I pray God that I am wrong in my suspicions, but I cannot ignore the fact that all of the strange, disparate pieces of events that have taken place only cohere when they revolve around Mary.'

'Like what?'

We were nearing a small park in the middle of the town, so I suggested we sit and rest on an available bench. 'Mary was the only one present in the house when her husband died. All this time I have assumed Graham's death was from natural causes, but now his body has disappeared from the morgue. I can think of one reason to steal a body: to prevent the police from determining *how* the person died, and that it was *not* from natural causes.'

'So how does she sneak the ol' boy out?'

'I don't know, but I would imagine that it would be easier for a spouse to gain access to a cadaver in police custody than it would for anyone else.'

Harry sat and thought for a moment, then said, 'Okay, ducks, let's say you're right and she spirited 'im away, and nobody's talkin'. Where does she stash the body?'

'If I had to guess, I would say in her home, which would explain why Mary was so willing to leave her house and come stay with me in the Tudor Rose. It wasn't that she was afraid to be alone, or because she feared someone was breaking into her home. It was to get *me* out of there before I discovered Graham's body!'

'But if she's afraid that the peelers are going to discover she's brown-breaded her mister, why'd she let 'em take the body in the first place? Why not just say she'd take care of everything, and then go quietly plant him somewhere?'

'Because it was not her decision,' I said

grimly, remembering the scene in the house in Bull Street right after Graham Chelish's death had been discovered. 'It was Inspector Islington who insisted the body be taken to the morgue, and at that moment Mary was hardly in a position to argue. Doing so would have raised suspicions in the mind of a Scotland Yard inspector. She had no choice but to play along and act the role of the grieving widow.'

'Why'd she have to go an' kill ol' Plummer, then?'

'Maybe Mr. Plummer figured out what Mary was up to and she had to silence him. Oh, heavens, maybe she was planning to kill him all along, and that's why she came to the Tudor Rose with me. She confronted Plummer, killed him, and then in trying to escape, encountered you returning from the town. Harry, maybe it was *Mary Chelish* who ran into you and knocked you over on the street, and then doubled back and returned to her room.'

'Blimey! But why'd she want to kill her husband in the first place?'

'That I cannot answer,' I admitted. 'Maybe she was driven to distraction by his erratic behaviour. Maybe it was some other reason about which I know nothing. There's one other question for which I also have no answer.'

'What's that?'

'How Professor Macnee fits into this,' I said. 'There has to be a reason for his murder, though I cannot imagine what it was, which leaves me little choice but to operate under the assumption that his death in London falls outside of the occurrences that have taken place here. Who knows? Perhaps it was Mr. Plummer who killed the professor.'

'Maybe he and the widow are in on it together,' Harry offered.

'That's possible, I suppose, though, it presumes that they knew of each other and — ' I ceased talking as a thought suddenly struck me. 'Oh, oh, *no*.'

'What is it, ducks?'

'What if the woman I know as Mary Chelish is not really Mary Chelish? I was only taking it on faith that she was the sister of my friend Beth, but what if this woman is no more Mary Chelish than Gordon Plummer was Professor Macnee, or my husband, for that matter, or than you are Hathaway Broughton and I am Lady Pettigrew?'

'Blimey. Who is she, then?'

'I don't know. But what if she were a confederate of Professor Macnee and Mr. Plummer, who decided to get rid of them? When Graham Chelish suddenly appeared at his home, he seemed stunned, confused. I took it for some form of mania, but what if he was confused because the woman pretending to be his wife was not really his wife? She would have had to kill him to keep him from telling anyone. But if that is the case, where is the real Mary Chelish? Harry, I need you to run back to the police station and find Inspector Islington. Ask him to come to the Chelish home as quickly as he can. I will be there to meet him.'

'Are you sure that's safe?'

'I'm not sure of anything at the moment, but please go.'

'Right,' Harry said, dashing off the

bench and trotting back toward the police headquarters. As he ran, I tried to figure out the most expeditious way to get a message to the Tudor Rose. Inspector Islington had told me they had a telephone, but I had not seen one. Even if they had, though, whence would I ring Mr. Price? As I stood pondering my problem, I spotted a young boy of about eight years strolling through the park. I decided to take a page from Sherlock Holmes's book of methodology. 'Young man,' I called, and the boy stopped and looked. I smiled as I approached him. 'Hello, I wonder if you would be willing to do something for me.'

'I don't even know you, lady,' the boy said rather rudely.

'Yes, I know, I am a stranger here. But if you will do something for me, there is a sixpence in it for you.'

The boy's entire demeanour changed. He pulled his cloth cap off with one hand while sticking the other one out to shake, and smiled broadly. 'Pleased to meet you, ma'am!' he said. 'My name's Toby.'

I took his rather soiled hand and shook

it, and then gave him quick but detailed instructions as to where I wanted him to go and what I wanted him to say once there, and then fished the coin out of my bag and handed it over.

'Like the wind!' he cried, dashing down the street, as good as his word.

As I had very little time to waste, I started toward Bull Street, hoping with each step that I knew what I was doing. Alas, by the time I actually arrived there, I was all but crippled with doubt about my reasoning and the rashness of my actions. Did I really believe that Mary Chelish was capable of killing three men in cold blood and then compounding it by assaulting Harry? Was she really so clever as to have spirited the body of her husband away, out from under the noses of the police? In the warm light of the Stratford day, it sounded like so much madness, and yet here I was approaching Bull Street.

A minute later I was standing in front of the Chelish home, realizing for the first time that in my zeal to solve this conundrum, I had not given thought as to how I would gain entry into the house. Having all but convinced myself that this was the most foolish notion I had ever had, compounded by the fact that I had invited Inspector Islington to partake of my idiocy, I started to walk away. Then I stopped, my mind having suddenly awakened to something that should not be there if the house were truly empty and locked.

It was a thin wisp of smoke emanating from the chimney. The fireplace had been cold upon leaving the house yesterday, so why was there a blaze now? Had Mary come back here after all? And if it was not she, then who was inside?

My curiosity having won the battle over my better judgment, I slowly walked back to the house, but not so slowly that my actions might look suspicious to anyone else walking down Bull Street. I had to find a way to get inside. Moving around to the back, I examined all the windows, all of which were closed and curtained, and tried the knob of the back door, which was, of course, locked. It was then that I saw the answer to my problem.

To one side of the house was an angled trap door that led to a cellar. Reaching down to the handle, I pulled on it and found it unlatched. Laying the door open all the way, I could see a half dozen steep stone steps going down into the ground. Leaving the door open in order to provide enough light to see, I carefully stepped down into the dark underground. In the earth-smelling blackness I could barely make out a tray of carrots, potatoes and turnips, and some other produce that I had a hard time identifying. Only when I picked some of the latter up and examined them closely did I realize they were not vegetables at all, but rather candles. If I'd had a match on me, I certainly would have put one of those to use.

The further I ventured into the cellar, the darker it became, and I had to use my hands to guide me for safety's sake, lest I find myself sprawled on top of a pile of coal. Several feet away, and above my head slightly, I could see a thin horizontal strip of light, which I interpreted as a sign that there was another door, under which illumination from the house was leaking. Proceeding very slowly and cautiously, my feet eventually came to another staircase, one leading up. Keeping my eyes on the strip of light as I ascended, I held my hands out in front of me until they came into contact with another doorknob, which I gingerly turned.

The door was unlocked. Opening it, I found myself in the kitchen, which was dim due to the curtains being drawn over the windows, but had enough light to see. Closing the door behind me, I proceeded from the kitchen into the living room, which was empty, but not devoid of signs of life; namely the small smouldering fire in the hearth. Upon examining it, I discovered that it had not been made from logs or kindling, but what appeared to be papers.

'Mary, are you here?' I called, but received no reply; at least not from a voice. There was a noise, however — a small rustle, and it appeared to come from the bedroom. Steeling my courage, I approached the door to that room, which was slightly ajar. 'Mary?' I called again, but no one answered. Pushing on the bedroom door, I creaked it open enough to see inside. I could make out a figure standing in the darkened room, but I could not see who it was. 'Mary, is that you?'

'No,' a voice said. Soon I saw a figure stepping out of the shadows and holding a revolver, which was pointed in my direction. I gasped — no; that is being overly generous. I had to struggle to prevent myself from fainting.

'You're supposed to be dead,' I whispered.

'I know when one is dead and when one lives,' Graham Chelish quoted mockingly.

17

'You are an enormously inconvenient woman,' Chelish went on. 'Do you know how much careful planning you have disrupted? Do you have any idea of the magnitude of problems you have created for me?'

The look of cold rationality in his eyes was startling, given that the last time I saw him he appeared to be unbalanced; and at that moment, the truth of the matter struck me. I realized that a vital clue had been out in the open all along; I had simply failed to see it.

'What a fool I have been,' I uttered. ''Defy the foul fiend.' That is a line of Edgar's from *Lear*, but not from Edgar in his own persona. It is spoken by Edgar posing as Mad Tom, *pretending to be insane*, just as you pretended to be mentally impaired so convincingly that even your wife was taken in.'

Graham Chelish smiled cynically.

'Yet you did Edgar one better,' I continued. 'You not only pretended to be insane, you also pretended to die. What did you use to depress your pulse and respiration? Morphine?'

'An opiate for the respiration,' Chelish said. 'As for the pulse . . . ' Keeping the gun trained on me, he slowly walked to the dresser beside the bed, upon which sat a candelabra. Striking a match on the wood, he lit its five candles. 'My family business is wax, which is such a versatile material.'

I was puzzled for but a moment, and then I understood. 'You coated your arm and neck with wax to cover the pulse beat, didn't you? That is why your wrist felt cold and dead.'

'When the wax is of the proper hue, texture and temperature, it can be safely painted on. It is remarkably effective.'

'Why did you stage your own death?'

Chelish regarded me as though I were a specimen in a zoo, and then said, 'You are a most surprising woman.' He raised his gun so the barrel was level with my eyes. 'Having a weapon brandished in your face does not appear to alarm you.'

'Neither does it delight me.'

'Even so, the threat of your own death makes you defiant, which identifies you as a person worth speaking to.' He slowly lowered the revolver so that it was now pointed at my midriff. 'I will do you better than merely explain my artificial demise. I will let you hear the plot you have toiled so mightily to complicate. Since you appear to be a perceptive person, particularly for a woman, I will give you the opportunity to identify any flaws so that I may correct them.'

'The first flaw was to insult me just now by diminishing my sex,' I told him.

He looked baffled at first, and then understanding dawned on his face. 'Ah, you are one of *those* women. Anything a man can do, you can do in less time, is that it?'

'I could certainly relate the details of a plot in less time.' In truth, I did not *want* him to rush through it. I wanted to keep him talking in the hopes that it would forestall his firing the revolver. I was, however, taking the risk that if I *appeared* to want him to get on with it, the result would be to make him draw things out, purely out of spite.

He smiled. 'We shall see how clever you really are. To answer your question directly, I staged my death because I was being threatened with exposure by a man I believed was loyal to me, a man who was in my employ. The only way I could protect myself in the short term was if Plummer thought I was dead.'

'*Plummer?*' I cried. 'Gordon Plummer was in *your* employ?'

'Oho, not so clever as you think, are you? Yes, he was in my employ. I hired him to find out what evidence that old fool from America had to support his theory that Queen Elizabeth wrote the works of Shakespeare. Plummer played his part well at first, ingratiating himself with Macnee and convincing him that he needed protection because of those threatening missives.'

'Which you wrote, of course.'

'Of course. Plummer gained Macnee's confidence and from that moment on never left his side, accompanying him to

London and acting the part of the dutiful protector, all the while keeping me informed as to Macnee's every move. His objective was to obtain the man's proof, which came in the form of a missive written by Robert Cecil. You do know who Robert Cecil was?'

'Yes. I heard all about the letter from Mr. Plummer.'

'I see. I was right, then, in fearing that he might not be the most professional operative money could buy. Once he and Macnee were in London, I received a telegram from him stating he was unable to get the letter away from the old fool, who kept it in a locked briefcase. It did not take long for me to deduce that Plummer had committed a cardinal sin: he had started to like the prey. As a result, he was becoming less insistent. Since I was already in Oxford at the time, I decided to make a short rail trip and take matters into my own hands.'

'You killed Professor Macnee.'

'I cannot say I enjoyed it, but it was the only way to obtain the letter.'

The fact that Graham Chelish was

readily admitting this did not bode well; it meant that, at least in his mind, I would not be alive long enough to relay these confessions to anyone. Still, I needed to keep the man talking in the desperate hope that Inspector Islington would shortly be arriving at the house, having been summoned by Harry. *Please, Harry!* I inwardly beseeched. *Please, get this one right!*

'I presume that Plummer realized you were the murderer, and that was why he had to be killed,' I said.

'Not at first, no. Plummer was genuinely shocked at the old man's death. I pretended to be as well, in addition to feigning anger that someone else had obtained the letter. When he mentioned some theatrical ham he had engaged to help him with Macnee's lecture, I persuaded him that *he* had killed the professor and had stolen the letter.'

Which explained why Gordon Plummer had followed us here to Stratford.

'It might have stood there,' Chelish went on, 'but for an act of carelessness on my part. During one of our secret meetings here, I left the professor's briefcase and the letter in plain sight. Plummer realized there was only one way I could have obtained them, and he threatened to go to the police.'

'So he had to go.'

'Yes, but first I had to murder myself. That bit of improvisation seemed to be the easiest way to prevent Plummer from carrying out his threat. After all, a dead man cannot be arrested. My demise, however, was intended to fool only Plummer. Then you showed up with that oaf from Scotland Yard, who insisted that my body be transported to the police station. That caused me no little panic, madam, and damn you for your complicity. The prospect of being examined by a police physician was also worrisome, though fortunately that did not occur. As soon as I had been left alone in the morgue, I rose up from the slab and escaped undetected. I sneaked back here only to find that Plummer had entered the bedroom and found the Cecil missive.'

That explained the mysterious break-in

Mary had reported.

'I had to get the letter away from him,' Chelish continued. 'Since I knew where he was staying, I had a note delivered to him. In the note I wrote that I was the Scotland Yard inspector who was presently haunting the town, and that I knew everything about the murder of the American. His only chance of escaping arrest, I wrote, was to surrender the Cecil letter to me. I told him when and where to meet me, setting the time in the middle of the night so no one would detect us, or so I thought. There were two others on the grounds at the same time, which prompted me to flee.'

And run straight into Harry, I thought, shuddering. 'You dropped your knife, you know,' I said. 'The police have it.'

'Good for them,' Chelish replied. 'All it tells them is that Plummer was indeed stabbed with a knife. It cannot be traced back to me.'

'Why is it so important that you get that letter?' I asked, changing the subject away from Harry.

'To destroy it, of course,' Chelish said,

as though that were the most obvious question in the world. 'I destroyed the professor's manuscript and other papers, and I was preparing to destroy the Cecil letter when I heard someone coming up the cellar stairs. I assumed it was Mary, but alas, it was you.'

I was not certain how much longer I would be able to keep the man talking, which made the impending arrival of the inspector most welcome at any time. 'Mr. Chelish, are you really such an egotist that you cannot allow any theory that competes with yours?'

'What do you know of my theory?'

'That balderdash about Cervantes having written the works of Shakespeare?' I probably should not be antagonizing a man who continued to hold a gun on me, but I was becoming annoyed with the lout.

Chelish's eyes narrowed. 'No doubt you learned of it from that water-fly at the Memorial Theatre.'

'From whom, I am told, you tried to steal materials that would have proved your theory to be so much tommyrot. Do you really expect to sway people into believing that the author of *Don Quixote* is also the author of *Hamlet*?'

'I don't care one way or the other. All that concerns me is getting back what is rightfully mine.'

'What is it that is rightfully yours?'

'Land, madam, land! I do not expect you to understand, but your assumption that I am nothing more than a blinkered scholar who is insanely jealous of competing scholars is a misconception I must work to counter, since it points a finger at my complicity in Macnee's death. Thank you for articulating it.'

'You are not welcome.'

'What's more, you have given me another idea.' He raised the gun barrel level with my head.

'What are you going to do?'

'For the moment, it is what *you* are going to do,' he replied. 'On the table over there you will find a piece of very old parchment. Retrieve it, please.' Since he was following me with the revolver, I moved at a glacial pace until I reached the table in question. I glanced down at the parchment, which was covered with faint writing that I was unable to read in the dimness of the room, and then picked it up.

'What do you want me to do with this?' I asked.

'You are going to burn it,' Chelish answered with alarming calmness and evenness. 'You see, what I plan to tell the police is that *you* are the blinkered Shakespearean scholar. It is *you* who killed Macnee and Plummer, and then you broke into my house, stole the letter, and tried to kill me as well; but you botched it, not realizing I suffer from catalepsy.'

'Catalepsy?'

'Yes, a disease that simulates the effects of death. I suffered a seizure right as you were attempting to kill me, so you thought you succeeded. Later I awakened in the morgue and found my way out.'

'Nobody will believe any of this.'

'Who is going to contradict me? Certainly not you, since you will be dead. Finding you in my house once again, I have no recourse but to shoot you.'

'You wouldn't.'

'Do not question my resolve,' Chelish said. 'I have come this far, and I cannot stop, I cannot go back. What's done cannot be undone. I will have what is rightfully mine!'

What in heaven's name did he mean?

'Go into the living room,' he ordered, and there was naught I could do but obey. Clutching the object for which two people had died, and for which I was in danger of becoming the third, I was forced to acknowledge that Inspector Islington was not going to arrive in time to rescue me. If I wanted to see the morning, I had to figure out some way to do it on my own. And if I could manage to do so without actually destroying this letter, which would stand in evidence should Chelish be apprehended and placed at the bar, so much the better.

With the barrel of the pistol pressed hard against my back, I was forced toward the fireplace, which contained a pile of smouldering, glowing embers. But then I saw something on the mantel shelf: it was another letter, this one on modern paper rather than parchment; but given the dimness of the room, it was a close enough match. It gave me an idea; perhaps not an idea that would save my life, but one, at least, that might save the vital piece of evidence I was carrying.

I suddenly stopped in front of the fireplace and tensed.

'What are you doing?' Chelish demanded.

'I heard something,' I lied. 'Someone is coming!'

As I had hoped he would, Graham Chelish turned and looked to the front door, even though he continued to keep the weapon pointed in my direction. It was just enough time to allow me to shove the purported Cecil document into the sleeve of my dress and then reach out and grab the paper on the mantel.

'I hear nothing, and I am losing patience!' Chelish declared. Turning back to me, he added, 'Now, move!'

I started once more toward the fireplace, now convinced that I had at least a faint chance of escaping a bullet. If I could distract him once more, get him to look away, I might have enough time to grab a fire-pit tool and try to disarm him. It would be a risk, but it was the only chance I had. Taking a deep breath and praying I was not imagining a fool's dream, I knelt down before the fireplace, the flames of which were now nearly extinguished. 'The embers are cooling,' I said. 'I do not believe this will burn.'

'Oh, for god's sake!' Chelish turned away, but not so completely that I had any chance of running. From a nearby table he grabbed a candlestick with a lit candle. 'Here, use this, and be quick about it!' he said, thrusting it toward me, blissfully unaware that he had just handed me the means of escaping him.

Holding the substitute letter in my left hand so as to maintain a firm grip on the brass candlestick with my right, I touched the corner of the paper to the candle flame and then tossed it onto the embers. As it started to go up, I steeled myself for what I had to do next, remaining conscious of Chelish's every movement. He was standing directly behind me, looking over my shoulder.

'Very good,' he said. 'I must now move

a ways back, so it will look like I just came in. Please do not be so foolish as to — '

He stopped speaking and froze as he saw the white paper blackening and curling. *'God damn you, what is that you are burning?'* he screamed so vehemently that I nearly dropped the candlestick. *'That is not the right letter!'*

His revolver all but forgotten, Graham Chelish dove for the fireplace, hand outstretched. It took no strength at all — at least I could not feel the exertion — to swing the candlestick up and into his chin. There was a sharp cracking sound, and then he flew backwards and crashed onto the floor. He made no move to rise back up.

At that moment, everything seemed to happen at once. As I withdrew the paper from the fire and tamped out the flame that had consumed about a quarter of it, the front door burst open, and a second later a woman's scream shattered the silence of the house. Following that, I heard duelling cries of 'An unforeseen development!' and *'Gor, blimey!'*

'What is Gray's body doing here?'

Mary shouted, rushing to the supine figure on the floor. 'Amelia, what have you done?'

'I am afraid I've proven that Gray is not quite as finished with his body as we imagined,' I replied. 'He is alive.'

'Oh, my god!'

Inspector Islington rushed over to the unconscious figure and examined him. 'How utterly remarkable! His pulse, which was absent the last time I examined him, has returned.'

'I will explain it to you later,' I said. 'But please, when he awakens, take him into custody. Near his hand is a weapon with which he attempted to kill me, hoping to make it look like self-defence.'

'Amelia, what are you saying?' Mary cried.

Believing that I had spoken it with the utmost clarity, I did not bother to repeat myself. Instead I withdrew the parchment from my sleeve and handed it to the inspector. 'He was trying to get me to destroy this document,' I said. 'But since it may have historical value in addition to being a key piece of evidence in this convoluted matter, I managed to conceal it. That scorched letter in front of the hearth is a document I started to burn in its place, and when he saw what I was doing, he reacted like a madman.'

'Let me see,' Mary said, coming over and picking up the ashy paper. 'This is a letter from Terrence Chelish. That was Gray's uncle.'

Before she could examine the letter more thoroughly, a moan came from Graham Chelish, whose jaw I sincerely hoped would never stop aching. Mary rushed to him and knelt beside him. 'Gray,' she said, 'Amelia says you tried to kill her. She is mistaken, isn't she? Please tell me she is mistaken.'

Chelish uttered something, the first word of which was *miserable*, while the second I believe was meant to refer to me, since the Chelishes owned no dogs, female or otherwise.

Inspector Islington stepped over him. 'Graham Chelish, how do you answer the charge from this woman that attempted to kill her?'

'I lost my wits momentarily,' he lied.

'You are no more insane than I am,' I rejoined. 'You were certainly sane enough to kill Professor Macnee and Gordon Plummer.'

Chelish had now struggled to a sitting position, and was rubbing his chin. 'That's nonsense,' he said.

'He confessed everything to me, Inspector.'

'Prove it.'

Mary Chelish, who had grown quite pale, now rose and held the letter from her husband's uncle in front of her. 'Amelia, you said that he acted like a madman when this was threatened with destruction?'

'Yes, he did, so much so that he momentarily dropped his aim on me. That was how I was able to fight back.'

'Then perhaps he will act like a truthful person now.' With that, Mary Chelish ripped the letter in two, and Graham reacted as though he was shot.

'Stop!'

Holding the halves together, Mary said, 'Is she right, Gray? Did you kill those people?'

'Mary, please . . . '

She ripped the halves in two.

'For God's sake, stop!'

'Tell me the truth, Gray!' In the tense silence that followed, Mary walked to a lit lamp and, protecting her hand with a fold in her dress, lifted off the globe, then held the paper close to the flame.

'No, please, don't!' her husband cried. 'Yes, I killed them! And I tried to kill her! Just don't burn that. It's all I have left.' Then Graham Chelish actually began to sob. For her part, Mary joined him, weeping silently.

I had all but forgotten Harry was present until Inspector Islington said, 'Mr. Benbow, would you be so good as to fetch the local constabulary?'

'Right, guv,' Harry said, dashing out of the house.

The inspector then came to me. 'Are you all right, dear lady?'

Was I? More than anything else, I felt numb. 'I shall recover,' I said, praying I was correct.

'The way you comported yourself throughout this ordeal was nothing less than astonishing, if I may say so.'

'You may. But please, Inspector, could you help me to a chair? I suddenly feel faint.' He did so, and I managed to retain my consciousness after I sat down; but with consciousness of this sort, oblivion suddenly did not seem all that bad.

While the Chelishes continued to weep, each for a different reason, and I fought to maintain my wits, Inspector Islington held the Cecil parchment close enough to the lamp to read it. 'My word,' he exclaimed after a few moments. 'For your brilliance in seeing that this document was preserved, dear lady, you should receive honours from the Crown.'

18

The George Inn
Bankside, Southwark, London
1603

The innkeeper pounded on the upper-room door so violently that Robert Cecil thought he might break it in two. 'Come on, Will,' the man shouted. 'There's someone here to see you.'

'Is it someone's husband?' a voice called from behind the door.

'No.'

Outside the door, the newly created Baron Cecil smiled. 'It is Robert, Will. Let me in.'

The sound of a door being unlatched was heard by both the baron and the simple innkeeper, at which time the latter said, 'I shall leave you now, m'lord.'

'Today, my good man, you have earned the gratitude of Robert Cecil,' the courtier told the innkeeper with a smile.

'God bless you, m'lord,' the innkeeper said, grinning and bowing so deeply that his chin all but scraped the floor of the gallery as he backed away.

If more of the general populace were this grovelling and obsequious, how functional the realm would be, Cecil thought.

Now that the door had opened, Robert Cecil swept in, alarmed by the condition of the room. 'God's blood, William, this room has not been cleaned since Agincourt!' he cried. 'It smells to heaven!' A bleating sound was heard, and Cecil saw a young goat dart by him, which at least explained the smell. 'Do I *want* to know why that thing is here?'

'He is the company mascot,' William Shakespeare replied. 'I have offered him room and board in return for companionship.'

'How can you live like this?'

'My mind is occupied by matters other than neatness. How fares His Majesty King James?'

'Very well. He remains shaken by the fact that Her Majesty died so soon after his private meeting with her, which is to say, of course, that he also remains ignorant of your skill as a feminine impersonator.'

Privately, Will Shakespeare continued to have mixed feelings about his command performance of Elizabeth Regina, for the benefit of the Scottish king, while Her Majesty lay dying in another room in the palace, though he knew to keep those thoughts private.

'Your performance was flawless,' Cecil continued. 'You convinced James that his succession was preordained by God, and helped drive away the few remaining fears he had been experiencing, while instilling in him resolve to fight the efforts of the Brookes and the Greys, who wanted to force my cousin onto the throne.'

'Your Catholic cousin.'

'Yes. But Arabella Stuart shall never reign, thanks to you. The plots have been detected and the plotters apprehended. By God, Will — even now, with your moustache and whiskers returning, you still resemble Her Majesty, rest her soul, with uncanny verisimilitude. Are you positive you can document your parentage?'

Shakespeare laughed and then struck a dramatic posture. 'How now, you grievous changeling!' he cried daringly. 'Dost thou profanely proclaim that Her virginal Highness whelped a bastard, and that I am that self-same wretch?'

Lord Cecil laughed heartily, not in the slightest offended by the words. 'You are someone's bastard, Will, though precisely whose I cannot say. Perhaps the theatre's itself.'

'Mayhaps you are right, Robert,' Shakespeare said, and then both men laughed anew. Then turning serious, he added, 'Tell me something, Robert — I must know. Had Her Majesty not been on her deathbed, had she been well enough to attend King James, rather than it falling to me, beclad in royal raiment and impersonating her, would she have agreed to everything that I bespoke to His Majesty?'

'You have my word on it, William.'

Will Shakespeare of Stratford became pensive, lowering his balding head and sighing.

'Something bothers you, my friend,' Cecil said. 'Tell me what it is.'

'You know, Robert, that my family is Catholic. I was born a Catholic, but for your sake, I have taken on a role that will ensure that this realm remains Protestant. I am not certain that I have been adequately compensated for what I have personally sacrificed on your behalf.'

'I have anticipated that, William. That is why I have brought you this.' Cecil handed a rolled parchment to the playwright, who opened it and read:

Let this missive bear witness to the vested union of playwright William Shakespeare and Her Majesty Elizabeth Regina, and let this Document by my hand testify that the two are one and the one are two, and should any man protest the one, he perforce protests the other, and woe be to him. So it shall be for the duration of the sovereign realm of England.

So I have written in my capacity of secretary of state, on this Twentieth day of August in the year of our Lord 1603,

Robert Cecil, Baron of Essendon,
Secretary of State to Her Majesty
Elizabeth R. and His Majesty James I.

'Very pretty, but what am I to do with this?' Shakespeare asked.

'For the service you have provided to Queen, King, country, and me, you shall immediately present this letter to any man who challenges you in any way, be it a legal matter, a matter of business, or a matter of faith,' Cecil said. 'Take note, William, of the latter, for whichever religious direction this realm may take within your lifetime, you and those around you will be protected by this document. This letter, William, is nothing less than perpetual immunity for you and your family against anything that may happen.'

Shakespeare regarded the parchment with newly opened eyes. 'My lord, I do not know what to say,' he uttered.

'Say that you shall never champion a Catholic revolt against the Crown, William, and I shall be satisfied.'

'I will sequester my religion from my

pen and my voice and keep it private, Robert. You have my word.'

'That is sufficient for me. God be with you, Will. You shall ever enjoy my patronage.' Cecil took his leave of the reeking, squalid room.

Will Shakespeare had never considered himself to be a double for Queen Elizabeth, but more than one person had casually remarked about such a resemblance, even before Robert Cecil had appeared backstage after a performance of *Hamlet*, in which he had enacted the role of the Player Queen. He had been alternately exhilarated and terrified by the appearance of Her Majesty's chief minister, who had presented him with a highly irregular proposition; but he had managed it, convincing the singularly unobservant James, who had only known Her Majesty from paintings, that he was she. The result of his performance was a monetary provision that would provide him with the means to retire back to Stratford and live the rest of his life in comfort . . . if Anne would have him back.

He remained convinced that she would,

in spite of his many indiscretions in the bedchambers of Southwark. If he could convince the King of England and Scotland that he was a virgin queen, certainly he could convince his wife that he was a devoted husband. Written poetry and playwriting was fine for the nonce, though none of it he felt was destined to survive the test of time; but Will Shakespeare was nothing if not a consummate player.

19

'This is fascinating,' Morland Greaves said as he examined the parchment that had cost Professor Macnee and Gordon Plummer their lives. 'Thank heavens you prevented Chelish from destroying this.'

We were in Mr. Greaves's cramped office in the Memorial Theatre building, which was made all the more cramped by the oversized presence of Inspector Islington.

'You believe it to be legitimate then?' I asked.

'If by that you mean do I believe it was written by Robert Cecil, then yes, I believe that it was. If, on the other hand, you are asking whether this is proof that Queen Elizabeth was William Shakespeare, I am much more sceptical. Cecil's letters are renowned for their deliberate misdirection. This one can be interpreted any number of ways. I could easily make a case for its meaning to be nothing more than a declaration that Queen Elizabeth and Shakespeare were of the same mind when it came to religious and political matters as I could that they were one and the same person.'

'So those people died for nothing?' I asked. 'Graham Chelish will likely spend his life in prison for a delusion?'

'He will not be the first to do so,' Inspector Islington said.

'You have not yet explained to me why Chelish was willing to kill for his deranged theory,' Mr. Greaves said.

'He said he was being denied what was rightfully his,' I replied. 'Whatever that means.'

'I believe I can begin to piece the answer together, based on my talks with the prisoner and a review of the charred and torn remains of that letter, which I was able to reassemble,' the inspector said. 'The tragic irony is that Graham Chelish cared not a whit who William Shakespeare may or may not have been.

This case from the very beginning was about land ownership.'

'Graham had spoken of land that was rightfully his, but at the time it made no sense,' I said.

'The sense of it was in that letter, the one you singed in the fireplace, Mrs. Watson. It was written by Chelish's uncle on his deathbed. The elder Chelish went to his grave believing that a local brewer named Charles Edward Flower, who donated the land upon which this very building we are in was erected, had cheated the Chelish family out of the acreage.'

Flower, I thought. Mary had told me that Graham had become obsessed with flowers, or a flower, but I took her literally. Once again the truth was there, in the open, and I had failed to realize it.

'I happen to know about that transaction,' Mr. Greaves said. 'This was definitely Flower's land. He gave it to the city for the purpose of creating a permanent monument to the memory of Shakespeare.'

Inspector Islington continued, 'But the Chelish family had previously owned this land, and at one point it had been proposed by the family as the site for a new candle works. Those plans, and any others that the Chelishes might have had for the property, were dashed when Charles Edward Flower obtained the entire acreage as collateral against losses sustained in a game of poker.'

'A poker game?' Mr. Greaves said, looking astonished.

'It was Graham Chelish's great-uncle Ralph who had made the wager and lost. Unable to accept the fact that he had sacrificed his sizeable patch of land for an insufficient poker hand, Ralph Chelish accused Flower of cheating at cards. He could prove nothing, of course. The other players in the game took Flower's side in the dispute. It took many years for Chelish to recover financially from this loss, and he remained an enemy of Flower's for the rest of his life.'

'The Montagues and the Capulets all over again,' I muttered.

'Chelish initially sought redress through the courts, and when that failed, he challenged Flower to a duel, only to be rebuffed. In time, Flower grew so weary of the antagonism that he decided to put an end to the conflict by giving the land in question away. So he deeded the land as the site of the Shakespeare Memorial, figuring that was the end of it. With hope of ever regaining the land now gone, Ralph Chelish soon died, a broken man. His son Terrence, who was the uncle of our murderer, and the man who wrote that letter, realized that pursuing the conflict was pointless, and instead worked to try and rebuild the family business. But then something happened to change his mind.'

Inspector Islington took what those in the theatre call a 'Macready pause', named after the actor famous for adding minutes to a performance through stillness. 'For heaven's sake, Inspector, don't leave us in suspense,' I said. 'What changed his mind?'

'Changing times, dear lady. Specifically, electricity. The candle business was already suffering because of new lighting sources, but then came this very structure, the Memorial Theatre, which became the vanguard of using electric lighting for its productions. That is correct, is it not, Mr. Greaves?'

'Yes, we pride ourselves on it,' the dramaturge said.

'As the candle business waned, Terrence Chelish increasingly became bitter about the fact that not only was this building erected on land that once belonged to his father, but that it stood as a visible symbol of the family's failing fortunes. Shortly before his death, he informed his nephew of the longstanding conflict and its significance, and it appeared to awaken something within Graham Chelish. He became obsessed with getting the land back.'

'But how could he?' Mr. Greaves asked.

'Ah, now that is where things become interesting,' the inspector said. 'In researching the matter, Chelish turned up a copy of the grant deed that Flower had given to the Stratford council forty years ago, which had been accompanied by a letter of instruction. The letter stated that the property was being given to the town to establish a theatre that would forever honour Shakespeare's memory, and — this is the part that inflamed Chelish's imagination — should the theatre ever fail in its designated task, the land would revert back to the Flower family. Were that to happen, the war over property could begin anew, with fresh challenges in court.'

'I can assure you, sir, the theatre has not failed in its designated task since I have been in its employ,' Mr. Greaves said.

'Of that, I have no doubt. But one must consider the mindset of our soon-to-be killer. In the absence of grounds to attack the theatre itself for shirking its responsibility, Chelish decided upon a more audacious approach. He decided to attack the reputation of Shakespeare himself by arguing that the man buried in Holy Trinity Church had nothing to do with the writing of the plays and poetry that bear his name. He decided upon the author of *Don Quixote* as the true playwright after discovering the coincidences of their deaths falling on the same day.'

'Yes, but I told him — ' Mr. Greaves began, but I cut him off by saying, 'Let us hear the inspector out first.'

'Thank you, dear lady,' Inspector Islington said. 'Chelish believed that if he could generate enough question regarding the authorship, he might convince the city elders that the purpose of the theatre was fraudulent, and the grant deed would be null and void.'

'That would not have happened,' Mr. Greaves said.

'Very probably not,' the inspector acknowledged, 'except in the mind of Graham Chelish, where the plan was foolproof. Until, that is, he learned of Professor Todhunter Macnee, who claimed to have proof that it had actually been Queen Elizabeth who had written the works of Shakespeare. Seeing that as a threat to his scheme, Chelish felt he had to get rid of the professor, which he did, and destroy the evidence, which, thanks to you, Mrs. Watson, he did not. When Gordon Plummer, who had been Chelish's confederate all along, realized the truth of the professor's murder, he signed his own death warrant.'

'Graham must really have gone mad, and not simply pretending,' I said.

'What is it Cervantes wrote?' the inspector asked. ''Too much sanity may be madness; and the maddest of all, to see life as it is and not as it should be?' I believe that is the quote.'

After a few more pleasantries, the inspector and I left the theatre building. But before leaving Stratford-upon-Avon altogether, there was a stop that I had to make, one to which I was not particularly looking forward. On the way to the Chelish home in Bull Street, I asked the inspector, 'What will happen to Graham?'

'Oh, prison, I daresay,' he replied, 'though the nature of his incarceration will likely depend on how sane he is judged to be. Will you return to London now, Mrs. Watson?'

'As soon as I am able. I must collect Harry first, and then will be on the next train.'

'May I say, dear lady, that you have been invaluable to this investigation.'

'Thank you, Inspector. I wish I had not been.'

He took his leave of me then, and I watched him lumber off into the distance before resuming my walk to Mary's house. I found her sitting in the front room, her head in her hands. 'Mary, I cannot tell you how sorry I am about everything.'

'Thank you, Amelia. Without you, I might not have got through any of this.'

'What will you do now?'

'I am going to visit Beth for the time being. Assisting with someone else's problems may help me get my mind off my own.'

'You know if there is anything you need, ever, you may call upon me,' I said.

'Yes, Amelia. If I know anything, I know that. And please say hello from me to your real husband. I hope he realizes what a lucky man he is.'

There were days when I also hoped as much.

Leaving Mary and arriving back at the Tudor Rose, I was rather surprised to find Harry waiting for me, wearing a new, if mismatching coat. 'Hello, ducks!' he cried. 'Ready t'go?'

'You seem in a chipper mood, Harry,' I said.

'That's 'cause I had a grand idea, Amelia! It's one that's gonna put ol' Harry back on the map!'

'You're not going to write a book, are you?'

'Nothin' of the sort. I'm gettin' back into the game. I'm gonna go back to London and start my own Shakespeare troupe!'

Oh, good heavens. 'Harry, that sort of thing takes money. You have to engage a theatre, hire a cast, a costumer, a stage crew . . .'

'Not a bit of it! I'll do one-man Shakespeare!'

'One-man Shakespeare?'

'Every part done by yours truly.'

'Every part.'

'Every bloomin' part in each ruddy play! Like splittin' meself into three! Or more.'

'Won't that make the swordfights a bit difficult?'

His ebullient expression suddenly disappeared, replaced by one of concern. '*Gor*, I hadn't thought of that.'

'You know, though, Harry, if anyone can figure out how to do a one-man swordfight, it is you.'

After collecting my things from my room, I settled the bill with Emrys Price, who appeared to still rue the absence of his niece. 'Please do not worry, Mr. Price,' I told him. 'I believe Glynis will be fine.'

'Aye, she'll be fine. But her father is on his way here to confront me. Will *I* be fine?'

'Make him one of your exquisite soft-boiled eggs and I am certain you will be.'

'God love you, ma'am,' he said.

Harry and I took a hansom to the train station, whence we would bid farewell to the place of Shakespeare's birth. Once we had settled into a second-class compartment, I was able to completely relax, perhaps for the first time since we had left London; so much so that I was in danger of falling asleep. Only when a bump on the tracks had jolted me upright did I realize that I had been nodding. 'Oh, sorry, Harry. I did not mean to nod off.'

'You are entitled to a bit of rest, dear lady,' a voice said, a voice that was *not* Harry's.

My eyes flew open and for a second I was startled by the sight of the intruder, but only for a second. 'Good heavens,' I said. 'Must you really haunt me like a bad memory?'

'My apologies, dear lady,' Inspector Islington said. 'I saw Mr. Benbow step out of the compartment, so I took this opportunity to talk to you privately.'

'What is it you want?'

'I would like to talk a business proposition over with you. I have watched you closely during our time in Stratford.'

'Don't I know it!'

'And I have been quite impressed with what I have witnessed. Let me come straight to the point: I believe there is a place for you in M Division, Mrs. Watson.'

'You must be joking.'

'Not in the slightest.'

Good heavens! Working directly with Mycroft Holmes, my distant cousin? What an outlandish idea! What would John think of such a scheme?

'You must admit that you have a rare natural ability for investigating, combined with a remarkable fearlessness,' Inspector Islington went on. 'Your skill as an actress is not only commendable but would be an asset to us, and I have witnessed your composure under duress and remain favourably impressed.'

I was grateful that he did not add *for a woman*. 'You were impressed even though I was not wholly truthful to you during the course of this case?' I asked.

'Mrs. Watson, anyone who can, as they say, pull the wool over my eyes, is someone I would prefer to have working on my side, rather than against me.'

'What would Mr. Holmes think of such a prospect?'

'I would not be making this suggestion without the guarantee of official support from my superiors.'

Oh, dear.

The inspector leaned closer. 'Mr. Holmes has known you and has watched you for a longer time than have I, and I can state without fear of contradiction that he would move heaven and earth to get you with us.'

'Good lord.'

'What may I tell him, then?'

'Tell him that there are more things in heaven and earth, Horatio, than are dreamt of in his philosophy.'

Inspector Islington smiled. 'Witty as always, but I did not hear the word 'no' in there.'

'Nor did you hear the word yes. I . . . God help me. I have to think about it.'

'I shall tell him, then, to await your answer.'

'Tell him I shall communicate with him at my convenience.'

The inspector smiled again. Then with no warning, the train entered a tunnel, casting the compartment into darkness. When it finally emerged, I discovered that I was alone. There was no sign of Inspector Islington ever having been there.

Harry returned shortly thereafter. 'You all right, ducks?' he asked. 'You look a little peaky.'

'It has been a challenging few days, Harry,' I said.

At last we pulled into Euston Station, and the two of us disembarked.

'Well, Amelia, we made it through another 'un,' Harry said cheerfully.

'Somehow,' I rejoined.

'Not somehow, luv. Because of you, that's how.'

'Do try to stay out of trouble, Harry.'

'Always, my girl!'

Oh yes, always. Harry turned and skipped away into the crowd at the station; and while part of me was sorry to see his sunny, if ill-fated, presence going away, I knew instinctively that I would be seeing him again soon, if for no other reason than to return his suit of clothes that I remembered were still residing in my hamper.

Outside the station I engaged a ride to Queen Anne Street, praying with every clop-clop of the steed that I would come home to a quiet, empty house. As it turned out, I did, though a letter in the post from John declared that his work in Geneva was nearly finished, and he and Missy would be home within the week. It also asked why we were still employing a maid who could not iron a shirt without scorching it. After laughing, I mentally answered, *Because we love her.*

Nothing to speak of happened over the course of the next two days, which was completely satisfactory with me. Rather than feeling confined by the silent stillness of the house, I now relished it. Then on the third day a letter arrived. That would not have been notable except for the fact that its envelope bore no return address or postage stamp. Opening it, I withdrew a single page and read:

> My dear cousin Amelia:
> I have asked our mutual friend Horatio to deliver this missal by hand.
> I am waiting on your convenience with eager anticipation.
> Will you join us, madam, and become a valuable asset to M Division? The Crown is most desperately in need of your talents, and I am most desperately in need of your reply.
> I await your response.
> MH

MH. *Mycroft Holmes.*

Since returning from Stratford, I had managed to convince myself that the mysterious conversation with Inspector

Islington on the train had been no more yielding but a dream; yet here was the evidence that belied it. Mycroft Holmes actually did wish for me to join him as an agent of the Crown, and was awaiting my reply.

Dear God in heaven.

At that moment I heard a voice inside my head; it was that of Sherlock Holmes.

Adventure is in our blood, cousin, the voice said. *You know that as well as I.*

I nodded.

'Yes,' I replied.

We do hope that you have enjoyed reading this large print book.

Did you know that all of our titles are available for purchase?

We publish a wide range of high quality large print books including:
Romances, Mysteries, Classics
General Fiction
Non Fiction and Westerns

Special interest titles available in large print are:
The Little Oxford Dictionary
Music Book, Song Book
Hymn Book, Service Book

Also available from us courtesy of Oxford University Press:
Young Readers' Dictionary
(large print edition)
Young Readers' Thesaurus
(large print edition)

For further information or a free brochure, please contact us at:
Ulverscroft Large Print Books Ltd.,
The Green, Bradgate Road, Anstey,
Leicester, LE7 7FU, England.
Tel: (00 44) **0116 236 4325**
Fax: (00 44) **0116 234 0205**

Other titles in the
Linford Mystery Library:

MOUNTAIN GOLD

Denis Hughes

Rex Brandon, internationally famous geologist, is flying to join a party of prospectors camped overlooking the frozen surface of Great Bear Lake in northern Canada, when his plane is forced down in a storm. Suddenly Brandon faces a 200-mile trek across the frozen wastes. Of the people he meets on his journey — all of whom want to get to Great Bear — several are destined to die, and Brandon cannot be certain that the survivors are who they say they are, or what their true motives may be . . .

WATSON'S LOST DISPATCH BOX

Gary Lovisi

Thomas Jones, a retired professor of English and rare book dealer, is astounded when a young man enters his shop offering an almost pristine copy of *The Strand Magazine* from July 1891, containing the Sherlock Holmes story *A Scandal in Bohemia*. But what shocks Thomas the most is that below the magazine title is a stamped inscription proclaiming in large block letters 'AUTHOR COPY'. Thus begins an astonishing adventure leading to murder — both past and present — and the discovery of Dr. John H. Watson's lost dispatch box!

BY WHOSE HAND?

Fletcher Flora

Guy Butler, Rex Tye and Ellis Kinder have three things in common. They're all nicknamed 'Curly', have all slept with Avis Pisano, and none of them love her. But now Avis is pregnant and desperate. She doesn't realize that Curly will stop at nothing to keep her out of his life — not even murder. But who is this Curly — alcoholic Guy? Mama's boy Rex? Or cold-hearted Ellis? Three stories of mystery and suspense from the pen of Fletcher Flora.

THE BODY IN THE CAR PARK

Geraldine Ryan

More crimes for Casey Clunes to solve. A body is found in a multi-storey car park, and by the sound of it, the deceased has antagonised any number of people . . . When a horse bolts at the local riding stables, and the body of a young girl is found, it looks like an unfortunate accident. But soon, further information comes to light . . . And in standalone story, *Deadline News*, D.I. Ed Bailey finds himself investigating a crime which hits close to home.